ARCHANGELS
Book I

CORINA ZURCHER

Nevermore Publications, LLC ®

www.nevermorepublications.com

Text Copyright © 2013 Corina Zurcher

Interior illustrations by Scott Edward. Copyright © NeverMore Publications, LLC

All rights reserved. Published by NeverMore Publications, LLC

Publishers since 2013

NEVERMORE PUBLICATIONS and the RAVEN LOGO are trademarks
and/or registered trademarks of NeverMore Publications, LLC

Library of Congress Cataloging-in-Publication Data Available

Library of Congress Control Number: 2016910969

ISBN: 0615755550

ISBN-13: 978-0-615-75555-7

Printed in the U.S.A.
Second American edition, July 2016

DEDICATION

This book is dedicated to my husband, Troy, for the countless nights spent without me. And to my parents: Gus and Marie, who have been my constant champions since this journey in the unseen world began.

"There will be the shout of command, the archangel's voice, the sound of God's trumpet, and the Lord himself will come down from heaven."
- 1 Thessalonians 4:1

PROLOGUE

"*My Father is wrong to do this.*"
"*God is never wrong, Lucifer.*"
Lucifer turned to face her; his cerulean eyes were filled with sorrow. He gently cupped his hands around her innocent face. "*You have eyes, but you do not see, Gabriel. You follow the wrong shepherd.*"

His hands fell away from her as he slowly turned to face the Great Waterfall pouring down from the throne in the kingdom of heaven.

"*And for that, my heart breaks for you, beloved. It breaks…for all of you.*"

*   *   *

Words from long ago. An argument that never ceased to die. A point still to be proven. How his words haunted her still. Clutching the golden ark in her long willowy arms, knowing the message of doom it carried inside, Gabriel was left with the question, *How did it come to this?*

"*Oh, Lucifer…*" She barely whispered his name and yet the cold wind answered her. It always answered her. The wind swirled around her ever so softly, caressing her. She closed her eyes willing it to leave her. But it remained, reaching out to her, running its silky fingers gently across her skin.

Gabriel looked down at the ark clasped tightly against her chest.

She had not moved in hours trembling at the thought of what she was about to do. But there was no other choice. It must be done. The time had come. It had been decided.

The cold wind gently blew through her raven hair, whispering to her, *"Beloved..."*

A look of torment flashed across her face at the sound of the melodious voice — *his* voice; hearing it brought her pain. The memory of Lucifer as he once was before he fell from the light was one that Gabriel had locked away from her mind for billions of years. But now the door had opened and it was his argument that she must remember, every word that he spoke she must cling to, every action she must embrace, for it was for him that she stood atop a dune of sand in the middle of the desert in the Eastern World.

"Gabriel..."

She opened her eyes at the sound of Lucifer's seductive voice. Looking down at the ark one last time, Gabriel raised her eyes to heaven and the archangel prayed.

THE TRUMPET

Forty years later...

"**D**OWN!"

Beelzebub and four other fallen angels answered the command of the cold wind. With their coal-colored wings, they dove out of the nighttime sky and landed in an orchard of dunes. Beelzebub immediately scanned the grounds gripping the hilt of his sword with his burnt scarred hand. He spoke a warning to the angels behind him, "Be on watch for Michael." The other four angels retracted their wings and gripped their weapons tight.

They marched.

Their jet-black wings combed the sand as they moved silently through the desert. On their two feet, each of the five beings stood over nine-feet-tall. Their bodies were human. Their spirits were not. Every line of their muscular form could be seen under the darkened soot that stained their skin, sculptures of anatomic perfection. Beings of the highest caliber of creation. Fallen Ones. *Angels.* Beelzebub, a pale-haired cherub, led them on listening for the voice on the cold wind — *Lucifer's voice.*

"*EAST!*"

The fallen warriors followed. Each angel shifted his eyes across the dunes, lifting them up to the starless sky, searching for any sign of forthcoming opposition. But even if it came, they were ready — for what they were about to do would bring down any angel from heaven faster than they could blink their red, scorching eyes.

"*STOP!*"

The cold wind suddenly slammed into them, holding them back from any further movement. Beelzebub looked all around for any sign of the archangels. All he saw was a vacant desert. He breathed a little easier as he and the fallen ones waited.

"*It is here…*" The wind swirled around them and behind them, forcing them into a huddle amidst a barren piece of land.

Beelzebub looked down at the pile of sand before him. Thinking about the object that lay beneath his clawed feet, he could barely believe what was buried below. *She would not do it. She hates him. For I remember it. I remember what he did to her.* Beelzebub shut his eyes, tensing as the vision of that long-ago memory bursts forth into his mind's eye. *Blood. Death.* The first memory of another angel's pain. He flinched as he remembered her still body, her brutalized form. His eyes burst open; he tried to shake off the feeling. *Lucifer must be wrong. He's been wrong before.*

It was the night before the war. The last night he ever knew what it was to live in the light. Gabriel had come to the rebel camp to plead with Lucifer. She begged him to make peace with God and come home. And for a moment, Beelzebub thought he would. He could see behind Lucifer's eyes that he wanted to, but when Gabriel had extended her hand to him, he turned on her instead. And the next day, the entire Angelic Host battled over their home in heaven.

Home…

How Beelzebub longed for his home. And after all these years of living in hell and roaming the earth, that relentless yearning for his paradise lost consumed all his action, tormented his every thought. When Lucifer told him he had witnessed Gabriel in the desert burying her most treasured gift from their Father, he could not believe it. She never let any angel come near it — only Lucifer. Only.

Ever. Lucifer. *"She let me touch her, Beelzebub, and she reveled in it. Gabriel has forgiven me. She is on my side once again."* If Lucifer was right about what Gabriel had done, his internal suffering would ease. The pain in his heart would be gone. *No more shadow. No more flame. To live in the light once more...*

Beelzebub breathed in long and deep, calmed by the very idea. Yes, if Gabriel had forgiven Lucifer, he and the rest of his brethren would be home — *soon*. But why would Gabriel help Lucifer now? Why would she forgive him? *She wouldn't.* There's only one way to know...

Huddling over the sand, the fallen angels waited. The icy breeze swept violently around them rising up like a tornado before plunging into the center of sand amidst their circle. The ground trembled beneath them; sand moved upon sand until an object could be seen emerging from below. The ground shook more violently as the object continued to rise up from its grave. All of the angels were silent as they looked to its resurrection. The sand fell away from the object and a golden ark emerged.

Beelzebub's eyes grew wide. Asmodeus, a Power, looked at him in utter shock. "It's true!"

Azriel, a Virtue, gasped in disbelief. "Gabriel's ark..."

Beelzebub remained silent, rapidly trying to decipher what he saw before him. His coal-colored eyes narrowed. *"Move."*

The fallen angels moved out of his way as he crouched down before the ark. The box glowed radiantly, covered in angelic script and symbols. Two skillfully molded cherubim were carved at each end keeping the lid locked in place. Two swords were crossed over their chests seemingly guarding the ark, daring anyone who opened it to await a battle as consequence.

Beelzebub read the angelic script engraved all across its base. The cold wind swirled gently around him as he translated the ancient tongue. His onyx-colored eyes darkened as he read the words. He did not speak them aloud. *Clever Gabriel. Not so helpful as Lucifer believes.*

As he continued to read, one of the other angels, Felix — a Throne — bent down beside it. Mesmerized by the intricate design of heaven's hand, he extended his scarred claw to touch one of the symbols etched in gold. Beelzebub caught Felix's movement out of the corner of his eye.

"DON'T TOUCH IT!"

With the swiftest of motions, Beelzebub wielded his sword and swiped it at Felix. Felix roared in agony, *"My hand!"*

Beelzebub looked from Felix to the rest of the warriors. They stared at their general in stunned silence. "The metal is cursed. Cover it."

Azriel secured a piece of cloth over the ark. Beelzebub looked down at the black severed hand lying in the sand. *No, not so easily done.* He looked up at the moonlit sky — not a single sign of heaven's arousal. *What are you up to, Gabriel?*

Felix slowly crawled toward his hand, gripping his arm in pain. He picked up his severed limb and cradled it in the crook of his wounded arm holding it tightly against his chest. He looked to his commander with hate-filled eyes.

Beelzebub's face was one of stone. "Better to lose a hand than your life." He shifted his onyx-colored eyes to Felix's bleeding wrist. "For the kingdom. For our prince."

Felix nodded his head slowly in understanding as his body trembled in agony. The rage behind his eyes slowly dimmed.

The cold wind moved all around the fallen angels. With barely a whisper, the deep melodious voice commanded them once more, *"Bring it to the mortal one."*

Beelzebub and the fallen angels bowed their heads to their unseen master and took flight into the night sky.

BELOVED RACHEL

England

"*After all this time…*" Rachel Devereaux was sitting in her apartment on her living room couch. She had been holding a present in her lap, staring at it, unable to open it regardless of the happiness and excitement she felt at its unexpected arrival. For the box wrapped in pretty pink paper with a large white bow also represented a great sadness to her, and that sadness overshadowed her joy rendering her body immobile. She had been staring at the package for the last half hour.

Rachel finally decided to move and, with nervous hands, lifted the small beige envelope. She opened the tiny card inside and quickly read its words:

I wanted you to have this to remember me by. Keep it safe.
- Dad

Dad.

How long had she waited for this — something so simple — a note, a gift, an outstretched hand from the one man in her life that had forgotten her the day that her mother died.

Sixteen years ago today, Rachel's mother Julia was buried in a box under the cold hard ground. Rachel had loved her mother; but her father loved her more. Julia was the light of her father's life — she was beautiful, smart, witty — *perfect* — a gentle spirit with a giving heart. And she was dead. Up until today, her father could be counted amongst the underworld as well.

When the package arrived on her doorstep, she wanted to throw into the trash. She wanted to be angry. She wanted to forget her father the way he had forgotten her. But she couldn't. She needed that package. And like the twelve-year-old girl she felt the moment she saw it lying on her front step, she grabbed hold of it and clasped it to her heart as if it were her father himself standing on that front porch.

Looking at the simple writing on recycled paper, the storm of emotions that Rachel had tried to hold at bay for the last half hour could no longer be held. They swept over her like a tidal wave pouring forth from the deepest depths of her soul. And there was no stopping it. She succumbed to the flood of heartache...*and wept.* She wept for the past; she wept for the present; she wept for the future that could never be regardless of the beautifully wrapped package that rested in her lap.

"Oh, god..."

Tears streamed down her face, falling upon the simple note threatening to wipe away any evidence of its words ever having been written. She frantically dried her teardrops. Rachel regained control of her cries and gingerly placed the card down on the end table beside her. She gently unwrapped the present, carefully lifting the taped ends of paper as if they were about to dissolve upon touch. After so many years of forgotten birthdays, this particular remembrance had suddenly shifted Rachel's world.

The phone in her flat rang. Rachel did not bother to answer it as she continued unwrapping her present, refolding the paper as if it were a delicate piece of lace. The answering machine clicked on and a cheerful, male voice could be heard in the background singing:

"Happy Birthday to you,
Happy Birthday to you,
Happy Birthday beloved, Rachel,
Happy Birthday to you!
'Tis I, Raphael. Wanted to remind you to
be dressed to the nines by seven o'clock this
evening. I am taking you to the best restaurant
in town. Bye, love."

Raphael. Rachel sighed deeply. She had completely forgotten. Actually, she hadn't, but she hoped *he* had. Rachel hated celebrating her birthday, but each year, without fail, Raphael made sure she did something special for the occasion. He knew her all too well.

Rachel checked the clock: 4:30 p.m. There was still time.

Wiping away the last of her tears, she set her gift down on the coffee table in front of her. Taking a deep breath, she opened the box and pulled out a brown, leather-bound case. It was old and worn. She noticed two strange symbols embossed on the outer casing — symbols that Rachel in all of her studies did not recognize. And she of all people would recognize them, for words were her passion. They were her profession. And she loved them. Old words. Ancient words.

Her pulse raced. *What is this?* Her heart pounded wildly as she untied the leather strap. Reaching inside, she pulled out a piece of old parchment. It was covered from top to bottom with the same unidentifiable symbols that were embossed on the front of the leather case. With trembling hands, she guided her fingers down the front of the paper. Rachel turned it over and found more shapes on the other side. *These are different.* Examining them, she took in their fluid, wave-like pattern as it continued all the way down the page.

Where did he get this? She narrowed her eyes and tried to think.

It had been months since she had spoken to her father. *Think, Rachel.* The last she had heard, he was on one of his archaeological digs somewhere in India. Rachel reached for the small white note and reread its words looking for any clue she may have missed.

Nothing. Not a single clue. Keep it safe. Safe from what?

Rachel looked at the symbols once again. She grabbed her phone and took a deep breath — the first one in over a minute. She dialed the number to a cell phone. The mechanical voice answered, *"The phone to the person you are trying to reach is no longer taking calls…"*

She hung up and dialed the number to a home:

"The number you are trying to reach has been disconnected or is no longer in service…"

She clicked off.

"This doesn't make any sense."

She tried one last number — the number to a corporate office — her father's office.

"You have reached the office of Dr. Jonathan Devereaux of Devereaux Enterprises. If you would…"

Rachel hung up. As she pondered her next move, a low hum suddenly filled the room. Rachel looked all around for the sound, but could not locate the source.

The humming grew louder.

Slowly, she turned her head and looked down at the parchment lying on the table. Taking in its foreign markings, Rachel extended her nervous hand and picked it up. Holding it, she could feel the slightest vibration; she could hear the magnifying hum. She brought the paper to her ear and listened closer. A cold breeze blew all around her head. It spoke to her, *"I…I…I…"*

Rachel recoiled at the sound of the whispery voice and quickly dropped the scroll back onto the table, terrified to touch it. The wind blew all throughout her flat causing the temperature in the room to drop. Wrapping her arms around her body, Rachel saw her breath fogging.

She quickly scanned the room. "What's going on here?" The wind was suddenly gone, disappearing as quickly as it came. The humming died down and the room grew eerily silent. Her breath, however, continued to fog.

Seeing her father's note in her lap, she reread its words, *Keep it safe.* Rachel's breathing quickened as she thought about her next move.

She swiftly grabbed the parchment, put it back in the leather case, and headed out her front door. The door slammed shut behind her. The note that came with the package fell to the floor.

Rachel's phone rang again.

From the shadow in the corner of the living room, there was a sudden shift of movement. The shadow came to life as it glided slowly across the floor.

It grew larger and larger until the form of a gigantic man emerged from the darkness. The shadowed being could barely fit inside the room as he stood at almost ten-feet-tall. The being crept slowly toward Rachel's coffee table as the answering machine clicked on:

"Hey, Rachel. It's Ben. I'm in town and wanted to know if you were free for dinner tonight. I know it's been a while, but I was hoping we could get together and talk. I miss you. Happy Birthday."

The answering machine clicked off. The shadowed giant stopped right next to the note lying on the floor. Bending down, the shadowed being picked it up and read its message with his emerald-colored eyes. The figure placed the note in the exact same spot from which it fell and whispered the words, *"After all this time..."*

MORTAL MAN

Rome

*T*o *have this to remember me by...*
He meant to say so much more to her — words of
understanding, explanation, pleading, but even those simple
words were difficult for him to write. He didn't know what else to
say. Jonathan Devereaux did not know what his daughter thought of
him, but if he were in Rachel's shoes, he would think nothing of him
at all. And that was not how he meant it to be. That was not the kind
of father he thought he would be. But that was exactly the kind of
father he had become.

Jonathan rubbed his temples vainly trying to calm his mind and
soothe the angst in his heart. But it was in his soul that his trouble
lied — and it was restless. Sixteen years had gone by, but there was
not a single day that he didn't ask the question, *Why did she have to die?*
Why did you take her away from me? And no matter how many times he
had asked it, he never got an answer. Well, he was going to get an
answer; his pain was going to be acknowledged...even if it was the
last thing he ever did. And there was one person who promised to
help him get it.

Keep it safe...

Jonathan still remembered the day when the invitation stamped in angelic language made its entrance into his world. It arrived in an old, brown leather case...and an angel delivered it. He had been overseeing an archaeological dig in India when the fallen angel approached him in the form of a man. The angel was tall, with long, pale hair. He called himself Beelzebub.

Beelzebub.

When Beelzebub approached Jonathan that night to explain who he was and what he wanted, Jonathan laughed long and hard. For who would believe such a thing? A man claiming to be an angel? And not just *any* angel — but a fallen one *from hell?* But as Jonathan laughed, he noticed that not a single flicker of movement escaped Beelzebub's pale face and muscular form. He didn't even seem to breathe. And those eyes — black as coal — they were eyes that held no life in them. They were as dead as a shark's. The most chilling of all was that those eyes never blinked as they looked at him. *Doll's eyes.* Looking into those pools of darkness, Jonathan stopped laughing. It was in that moment he *knew,* in the core of his soul he knew — *it was true.* Beelzebub was who and what he said he was. And Jonathan was suddenly seized with terror as he looked upon the fallen one. It took all of his courage to speak the words, "What do you want?"

"You hate God."

And there it was. His feelings spoken out loud by an immortal being who said it as simply as one would say "hello."

"No, I..."

"Mortal man, I have existed before the beginning of time. I have seen billions of men and women leave this world the same way they came. Some honor their Creator. Some never think upon Him. And some think so much about Him with their anger and pain and rage that their hate marks their souls and taints them with darkness. Your darkness in the light is a marker in our kingdom. *We...see...you.*"

As he spoke, Beelzebub's eyes never moved. His voice never rose, and it never fell. "You have something in common with our prince, mortal man. And for that I have been sent. The Prince of Hell offers you his hand to help you get what you have wanted all these years: justice. *Vengeance.* An eye for an eye. Your desire is the brand on our shields as we look to a heaven that is no longer our own. *What...say...you?"*

And there it was — a choice. A full exercise and test to that notion called "free will." *What say you?*

Vengeance upon God. Yes...the desire of his broken and bitter heart. *Make God pay. Make God answer. Make God understand.* Could he do such a thing? Now that the opportunity had presented itself, would he *really* do it? Did he still want to? And the answer to such a question was...*yes.*

How he wished he had chosen a different answer than the one he had chosen then. But it was too late. Bearing the heaviness of his heart now that it was weighed down with regret, all Jonathan could do now was think and wait.

Dr. Jonathan Devereaux stood before a large hearth in a hotel room looking worn and spent. He was a man in his late fifties with sad, hazel eyes. Silver kissed the temples of his dark brown hair that framed his highly intelligent face. He was a man deeply respected in the archaeological world for his passion, knowledge and limitless zeal on his quest for answers to the questions that plagued the human mind. And for that, Jonathan would be remembered throughout history for the countless artifacts he had discovered and the truths to various myths he had put to rest. But it was not his mark on the scientific world that Jonathan wished to be remembered — for there was only one person in the world he wanted to leave a good, lasting impression upon — his daughter Rachel.

Even if Rachel kept the scroll safe, would it be enough? Could her action redeem him? But how could another's action redeem your own? And then he remembered...

There was only one other being in the world that could shower him with mercy if Rachel could not. Even now, such an idea that he could be forgiven for what he had done lifted the weight from his heart just a little. But it was a principle he never understood but so wanted to believe in. *Believe it.* And so, standing in a hotel room all alone, Jonathan made another decision by the use of his will. He breathed deeply and lowered his head in silent humility. Moments passed before he could find the courage and voice to speak His name. *"God..."*

At the sound of God's name, the hearth suddenly exploded in dark blue flames. *"I...I...I..."*

Jonathan jumped back. Even with the sapphire flames roaring from the hearth, his breath fogged on the air. The cold meant only one thing: *a fallen one was near.* Jonathan didn't even bother to turn around as he spoke to the shadows, "You found it."

Beelzebub and the other fallen angels emerged from the darkness carrying a covered rectangular box. Jonathan closed his eyes. *The ark of the archangel.*

Jonathan finally turned and faced the fallen ones.

Watching as Beelzebub glided toward him, Jonathan wondered what the angel must have looked like when he resided in heaven. To watch this powerful being stride toward him with the footsteps of maliciousness and rancor, Jonathan wondered what kind of angel he used to be to get to this place where he led an army in hell. To see the blackened cherub wings, the long pale hair, the dark onyx-colored eyes, the burnt ashen skin, Jonathan wondered if that was what his own soul looked like — tarnished and marked with a mutated heart filled with toughened scars of pain. And if that were true, why on earth would God welcome such decrepitness into his kingdom? It would be a tragedy to bring such filth into the light. And with that single thought, Jonathan knew that where he was going on his death was a place he did not want to be, but one where he must surely go.

Beelzebub laid the ark down in front of him. The other fallen angels surrounded Jonathan anxiously awaiting the unwrapping of this great find. Jonathan could barely stand the smell of their burnt flesh and sulfur-filled wings carrying the stench of the dead. He covered his mouth as he untied the rope around the sandy cloth. The fabric fell away to reveal the golden ark. Jonathan gasped at its beauty as the archaeologist within emerged from behind his weary eyes. The box glowed radiantly, covered in angelic script and symbols — identical to the ones on the parchment he sent to Rachel.

Looking upon the box with its supernatural carvings, Jonathan glimpsed a piece of what greater majesty heaven itself must hold, and with that thought came the great torment in knowing that he would never see it. It was not until this moment that the weight of what Jonathan had done impacted him to the point of panic. And yet, he remembered that he tried to do right. He tried to find a way to change things — and he found it through his daughter. *Make it right, Rachel.*

Fully aware that he must not give any of his thoughts or emotions away, Jonathan played the game the only way he knew how — by playing on. He ran his hand across the ark's symbols. He asked Beelzebub, "What do these symbols mean?"

Beelzebub read the angelic language, *"This is the ark that bears my trumpet…"* He was interrupted by the blaze from the fireplace in the suite. Everyone in the room turned toward the blue flames.

The whispery voice spoke from the hearth. The flames danced upon each syllable, *"Open it."*

Jonathan hesitated.

The fire exploded, *"NOW, JONATHAN!"*

The skin underneath Beelzebub's eyes darkened. "Do it."

Jonathan took each of the cherubs' two swords and moved them together so that they matched up in one vertical motion. The ark unlocked. The sound in the room was so quiet that not even the crackling from the fire could be heard. Jonathan lifted the lid and dipped his hands inside. Beelzebub and the other four angels slowly backed away from the ark. They knew what was coming.

Slowly, a golden instrument emerged — a golden trumpet. Even from its design, Jonathan could see that this was no ordinary trumpet. It was carved from God's hand — simple, yet powerful to behold. He absorbed the intricate carvings from heaven's architect. Never before had he seen such craftsmanship — and he never would again.

Jonathan whispered, "The Trumpet of Armageddon."

He examined the instrument from all sides. It was perfectly crafted with its flowing form, rounded out at the end like a ram's horn. As he turned it around for closer view, the fallen angels moved out of its path careful not to be touched by its metal. There was a single inscription that spiraled down the horn. Jonathan turned toward Beelzebub, "Tell me what it says."

He held it out for Beelzebub to translate. *"Property of Gabriel. If found, please return to heaven."*

Azriel cackled in reply. The moment Beelzebub's coal-colored eyes landed on him, he choked on his own laughter.

The silky voice spoke again, *"Play the first tune, mortal man."*

Jonathan dared not move. His brow was drenched in sweat as he continued to stare at the instrument. His body trembled uncontrollably, racking in fear over the next moment that was about to come.

They must never find out. Rachel, keep it safe.

"Where's the scroll?"

Jonathan looked at Beelzebub. He swallowed hard. "The tune has already been memorized. I've practiced it often enough the way the Lord of Hell has taught me."

The burnt skin around Beelzebub's neck tightened in rage, *"There's more than one tune!"*

He lunged at Jonathan. Jonathan reacted instinctively and swung the trumpet in Beelzebub's direction. Beelzebub jumped away from him before the instrument's metal touched his skin. Several moments passed as they stared at one another, each despising the other. Beelzebub's skin loosened as he tried to calmly speak, "Where is it?"

A small defiant smile crept onto Jonathan's face. "I burned it."

Beelzebub merely stared at Jonathan with his lifeless eyes. A shiver ran through Jonathan's veins. Yes, those were the eyes that he knew…the eyes of death.

The fallen angels closed in behind their leader. The looks on their faces was lethal.

"Beelzebub…" The musical voice spoke again.

"Yes, my prince."

"His daughter has it."

Jonathan quickly turned his head toward the fire.

"Send one of our brothers. Take it from her."

Jonathan's face fell as he realized his ruse was all in vain. He closed his eyes in despair.

"Yes, my prince." Beelzebub nodded to Felix. "Go."

Felix bowed and disappeared into the shadows of the room. Beelzebub turned toward Jonathan. "It's too late to try and redeem yourself, Jonathan." He stepped a little closer; his face softened and, for a moment, Jonathan could see a flicker of Beelzebub's former self revealed behind his onyx-colored eyes. Beelzebub spoke lowly, "You cannot go back — no matter how much you want to."

"Play it, Jonathan!"

The flames danced all over the hearth.

Beelzebub whispered into Jonathan's ear from behind, "Play it or *I* will visit your daughter myself and drive her to madness. She has no faith. Her will is weak. It will be easy."

Jonathan's body was soaked to the bone in sweat. "Leave her alone."

Beelzebub continued, "Your daughter's marker flickers in the dark…*I…see…her…*" A cruel smile spread across the fallen angel's face.

Jonathan was shaking so violently, he could not control his hands as he brought the trumpet closer towards his mouth. "This is not what I signed up for."

Beelzebub responded, his voice sounded almost sad, "Welcome to my world. *Now play.*"

Jonathan brought the trumpet to his lips and blew.

ANGELS EXIST

Oxford University

Rachel was on her computer scouring through scans of old photos, publications and artifacts looking for anything that could possibly resemble or reference the scroll that had now come into her possession. Books and papers were strewn all over the office as her frantic hunt for its origin had taken hold of her every fiber. The only light in the office was coming from the bluish glare off her computer screen. The door to the office creaked open. Behind her, the outline of a tall, thin man stood in the doorway. Rachel didn't bother to turn around.

"Don't be angry with me, Raphael. It couldn't be helped." The door slammed shut.

"Oh, *really?* You couldn't pick up the phone or leave a note on your front door saying, 'Raphael, something extremely unimportant came up. I'm at the office having a pity party about turning a year older, feeling old, although I'm still young.' That sort of thing. Because *that* would have been the courteous thing to do — *polite* even!"

She continued to page through the documents on her computer. "I'll have you know that something extremely important did come

19

up. I can have a pity party any time I want to; and a person is only as old as he or she feels; and I feel old, therefore, *I am*."

Raphael stepped further into the dimly lit office. He was a young man in his early thirties, dressed in a finely tailored navy suit, white shirt, and silver tie that accentuated his onyx-colored hair and gray eyes. On a normal day, his eyes would shine with laughter, for one would often find Raphael smiling for no other reason than he enjoyed doing so.

Both Raphael and Rachel shared the moderate-sized office at the university, for they were colleagues — professors in linguistics — working jointly on researching the evolution of language amongst common species. He was an extremely handsome man in the classical sense: a paradox of beauty marred by an overly analytical brain that gave him an air of intimidation. And Rachel *might* have been attracted to him if it weren't for the fact that his obsessive-compulsive behavior regarding tidiness, efficiency, and his incessant need to organize everything his eyes fell upon, didn't drive her insane. The current look of horror on his face as he looked around the current state the office was in was confirmation that a love between these two would never be.

"What have you done?!?"

Aghast would have been a mild word to describe the tone in his voice. Rachel swiveled around in her chair to face him. With an innocent look on her face she answered, *"What?"*

Raphael pulled a handkerchief out of his jacket and started wiping the lenses of his glasses as if by doing so he could erase the appearance of the room with a single sweep of his cloth. Placing the glasses back onto his face, he blinked rapidly, willing himself to believe the picture in front of him was not what he was actually seeing.

"Rachel, I have carefully categorized, numbered, colored and sorted all of these books *alphabetically*!"

He picked up a few of the textbooks from a nearby chair. The stack itself closely resembled a Jackson Pollock painting — an arrangement of color and splatter represented by a frenzied emotional state of its creator. Defeated, he tossed them down upon a mountain of papers. The papers slid down to the floor in a landslide — mocking him.

"Look at this! You have utterly *destroyed* my system! Do you have any idea how long this is going to take me to recreate!?!"

"Probably as long as the last time." He looked at her, clearly not amused by her lack of concern.

"Well...*yes*! What are you even looking for?"

He tried to cross the room to look at her computer screen and stumbled over another pile of books. *"RACHEL!!!"*

"Hey, careful! I was looking at those." Raphael let out an exasperated sigh. Rachel reached down and picked up one book in particular and started flipping through it.

"My father..."

"He called?"

"No..."

"Stopped in for an overdue surprise visit?"

"Will you let me finish?" Raphael crossed his lean arms across his broad chest, silencing himself. Rachel looked down at the book in her hands and shyly replied, "He sent me something for my birthday." She set the book down beside her. Knowing the history of the long-forgotten relationship between Rachel and her father, Raphael soon forgot about the tornado in the room and focused on the one about to funnel down upon Rachel as he saw the wall that guarded her heart slowly crumbling.

"Oh Rachel, that's wonderful..."

She nodded. "Yeah, it was surprising. I'm still trying to process it. But what's more surprising is what he sent. I've never seen anything like it. I've been here for hours and am no better off than when I left my apartment."

When she did not say another word, Raphael chimed in, "Am I allowed to speak now?"

She rolled her eyes. "Yes, Raphael."

"So, if I may, you mean to tell me that the dinner reservations that

took me four months to get — in addition to a bribe to the maître d`
— were all for naught because you couldn't wait until *after* dinner to
find which store your father bought your present?"

"You…"

"And in so doing, you've caused this hurricane in the office, hurt
my feelings…"

"Raphael…"

"Sometimes, Rachel, I don't understand you." He sat down in his
chair; his shoulders slumped in disappointment. "I even look nice
tonight." He blew his nose into his handkerchief. "You know I'm
allergic to disarray."

Looking at her friend in his overly dramatic state, Rachel couldn't
help but smile. "I'm sorry, Raphael. I should've called. It was lovely
of you to remember my birthday. Thank you." She leaned over and
kissed the top of his head. "And don't worry. *I* will clean up this
mess."

"All right, you're forgiven. So what is this gift that's got you all
worked up?"

Rachel slid some papers off of her desk. Raphael cringed the
moment he saw them hit the floor. "Come here."

He walked over to the desk and saw the scroll spread across it. The
moment he saw it, the color drained from his face. He slowly
removed his glasses; his handkerchief fell to the floor. Rachel did not
catch his look; she was too busy looking at the document.

"It's…well, I don't know what it is." She panned her hand across
the symbols. "I can't identify these hieroglyphics. Even the symbols
were foreign to *me* at first."

Raphael's eyes rapidly scanned the document moving from left to
right. "Have you tested the paper?"

"Yes. The test indicated that it's about forty years old." She shook
her head. "I know this isn't a fake. This is something much more. I
can *feel* it — literally. It has a sort of hum or vibration, like it has a
soul of its own; kind of creeps me out. I thought I was going crazy in
my apartment. I thought I heard it speaking."

He looked up from the scroll. "What did it say?"

She laughed nervously. "You're going to think I'm nuts."

"What did it say, Rachel?"

She hesitated. "I thought I heard, 'I...I...I...' or something like that."

"For the kingdom..."

"What?"

Raphael collected himself. "Nothing."

"Anyways..." Rachel looked longingly at the scroll. "I can't stop looking at it, touching it, wanting to know everything about it." She continued to gaze at the paper with adoring eyes. "There's something extraordinary about this piece of paper."

"And your father, who has barely spoken to you in over a decade, suddenly decided to give you *this?*"

"Raphael, he knows how much I adore antiquities — almost as much as he does. I just don't like all the dirt that's involved — all the digging."

"One would never know by the state of this room at this moment."

She ignored him. "After all this time...he remembered. "He sent me a note. It said, 'To have this to remember me by. Keep it safe.'"

Raphael narrowed his eyes as he tried to decipher its meaning. She caught his look.

"I know what you're thinking, Raphael, but please let me have this moment to enjoy this gesture. Even if I am reading more into it than I need to. Even if it's just a simple gift. I *want* it to be something more."

"You may just get your wish..." He looked up at her. "Have you spoken to your father about this?" He noticed the wrinkle of worry that had planted itself in the middle of her forehead. "Rachel, what's wrong?"

Her voice softened. "I haven't been able to get a hold of him. And all I can do is search for answers to my questions without any concrete chain that links all of them together." Rachel turned back to her computer screen and started scrolling through the scanned photos once again. "'Keep it safe,' he said. I'm a person who loves languages, and yet his choice of words brings me no comfort." She sighed. "Nothing. Not a single clue." She sat back in her chair. "Until my father tells me where he got this, it's almost as if it miraculously appeared in the world."

"Those are not the words I would have used."

Rachel finally noticed the grave look on Raphael's face. "What are you thinking?"

He paused a moment before answering, choosing his words carefully. "I'm thinking that I wish I knew your father better."

Rachel scoffed. "Yeah, you and me both." She picked up the book she was flipping through and opened it to the section she was looking for. Rachel handed the book to Raphael and pointed to a symbol on the page. "Now, look. This symbol here is the symbol that represents the archangel Gabriel."

"What book is this?"

"One on Kabala. Stop interrupting. Now, it's used over and over again in the document." She pointed to the parchment identifying the same symbol that appeared in the book. The entire time she did so, Raphael's attention was not on the paper but on Rachel's face. "But, this one here..." She pointed to another symbol on the document. "This one is used the most, but I can't find it anywhere. That's what I've been looking for up until you walked in." With a single huff, she went back to flipping through her book.

Raphael looked at her for a long time. He knew the moment he stepped through the office door that something was wrong. The feeling of uneasiness crept up on him the moment he saw the darkened room. It was a feeling of angst. A feeling of despair. A feeling of someone watching from behind the shadows in the corners of the room but not really being there, and yet feeling that they were there all the same. He could feel the negative energy swirling around the room like an invisible black hole whose only desire was to suck everyone down. And the office...aside from it looking like a cyclone had ripped through it...the room itself was freezing cold. And yet...Rachel hadn't noticed. She hadn't noticed much these last four years. And now it was time to awaken her. It was now time to open her eyes and make her see.

Raphael took a deep breath and spoke the word, "Trumpet."

Rachel barely heard him. "What?" She kept flipping through the pages in her book.

"It's the symbol for trumpet."

She stopped flipping and looked Raphael directly in the eye. "Are you sure?"

He nodded. "I'm sure."

"I must have missed it in here. You recognize it? Where did you find it? How do you know?" She went back to searching for the symbol in her book. Raphael put his hand on hers, stopping her search.

"You didn't miss it, and you won't ever find it. It's not in any book of any kind."

Rachel eyed him. "Then how on earth do you know that that means 'trumpet?'"

Raphael looked her dead in the eye. "Rachel, you *are* right. I do recognize it...in more ways than you know." He breathed deeply. "This document is neither a fake nor a joke, though I wish with all my heart that it were; it *is* something far more. This document is a script — a script written by an angel. These symbols are the written words of their language."

Rachel merely stared at him. After a few minutes of awkward silence, she nodded. "Okay, Raphael..."

"Rachel, listen to me..."

She tossed the book down to the floor; there was a hurt look in her eye. "You know, Raphael, this actually *means* something to me."

"I know."

"No! You *don't* know! And I don't appreciate whatever it is you're trying to do." Her anger rose. "Do you know how long it's been since my father acknowledged that I *had* a birthday? No, better yet...*remembered* that I was his daughter and not just another colleague or some artifact he found on a dig?!?" Tears stung her eyes. "Not since I was twelve! *Twelve!* Sixteen years have gone by and, for whatever reason, my father chooses *today* to remember!" She looked down at the scroll. Her face fell from anger into sadness. "And I can't reach back because I don't know where he is." She gently touched the paper.

Raphael looked pained as he watched her. She looked up at him. "This document is the only piece of my father I've had in sixteen years."

"Rachel, listen to me. I know how much this means to you."

"Do you? This is precious to me, Raphael. Can you understand that?"

"If you think I'm making fun of you, I assure that I'm not. Your feelings..."

"My *feelings*..." She shook her head. She turned the scroll over. "If you know so much about these symbols, what about the ones on the back?"

"Rachel..."

"Well?" She looked at him challengingly. The moment Raphael saw the symbols, his jaw tightened. "They're music notes. There are seven different tunes here."

Rachel studied his face.

"And *you* recognize this..."

"Rachel..."

"Leave."

Raphael touched her shoulder. She threw him off. *"Leave!"*

He didn't move. Rachel merely stared at him for the longest time trying to figure out why Raphael refused to submit beneath this ridiculous argument to the point of disappointing her. He was the only man in her life she could depend on. The day Raphael came to the university four years ago changed her life forever. He was more than just a colleague; he was her very best friend. And although he drove her nuts sometimes with his overly obsessive desire for cleanliness, she loved him. He was the most honest person she had ever known. He had never lied to her before and she knew he was not lying to her now, which was why she was deeply troubled — for he truly believed the words he had just spoken. Thinking fast and hard about their conversation that led up to this moment, she backtracked to where the conversation took a turn.

"Why did you say you wished you knew my father better?"

Raphael paused before answering. "Because I believe the kind of man he is reveals the motivation behind his present action in sending this to you."

"Damn it, Raphael! Maybe he just sent it to me because he knew I'd like it!"

Raphael suddenly ripped the parchment from her hand; his silver eyes were wild with fury. "NOT *THIS*, RACHEL!"

Rachel was stunned never having seen him this angry before.

He turned his glowing eyes to the document and read, "In the year the antichrist was born, the archangel Gabriel took her trumpet bestowed upon her by God and buried it in the Eastern Desert. Her trumpet was sealed in a golden ark from heaven, protected by engravings of powerful cherubim. No other angel can touch the trumpet as long as it is encased in the ark. Only a mortal can open the ark and play the trumpet's tune." He tossed the paper back onto the desk and looked at Rachel, finishing the translation, "*All they need do is call upon my name to guide them to it.*"

Raphael turned his back on her trying to streamline his thoughts and simmer his emotions. He could barely breathe as the hammering in his chest quickened by the words written on that single piece of paper. Speaking them aloud had fueled a fire within him that he had not felt in centuries. And it was not just a quickening of emotion. He could feel the heat within his heart rising. And it was rage. It was fury. *That scroll should not be here. It should not exist.* And yet, there it was: resting in his office sent to be carried in the arms of his dearest friend on earth.

"Raphael…"

He turned and saw the look of fear on Rachel's face. "I'm sorry,

Rachel..." It was then that he heard it. He could hear the hum. His body went stiff as the humming grew louder. He heard the words, *"I...I...I..."* Raphael's jaw tightened.

"I'm not crazy." Raphael quickly looked up at her. "You hear it too. Raphael, what's going on?"

The look on his face was one that Rachel had never seen before. Gone was the softness around it that had always given him his innocent, boyish look. Instead, the comforting gentleness that Rachel had always seen behind Raphael's eyes had been replaced by a hard look of determination and a deep knowledge of something buried deep within the confines of Raphael's mind that had suddenly crept forth. She saw his clenched jaw, now clearly noticing the outlines and perfect carving of his very masculine face. Rachel picked up his glasses knowing full well that he could not see a thing without them; and yet, he was reading...flawlessly. Rachel's body suddenly went cold. In a matter of minutes, the brainy and nasally Raphael she had always known had suddenly become...*fierce*.

"Your father did not find this scroll on any archaeological dig." His silver eyes bored into her, "That document would never be buried! It is an open invitation, beckoning anyone to heed its word. This parchment was freely given to a willing taker — your father."

"Stop it. Angels don't exist, Raphael! They don't!" Raphael's face tightened. "Don't look at me as if you suddenly believe in them! Last time I heard they were mentioned in scripture and haven't been heard from since. They're folklore — mythical creatures civilizations made up so that they would feel less alone in the world; ones weirdo esoterics idolize! You *know* this!"

Suddenly, a loud crash filled the entire office. The ceiling smashed down upon them...and Felix fell through the ceiling.

Raphael roared, *"My office!"*

Rachel screamed as the fallen angel rose and looked at her with his red, goat-like eyes. Raphael grabbed her and pulled her behind him to protect her. Felix saw Raphael and sneered with his low, gravelly voice, *"Raphael!"*

Raphael lunged at the fallen angel. They collided into one another and smashed into the far wall knocking over the bookshelf. Raphael was on top of Felix. He took advantage of his position by slamming his fist into the demon's face.

Rachel looked up at the hole in the ceiling and could see the night sky up above. More debris fell from the ceiling and onto Rachel. She cried out in fear, *"RAPHAEL!"*

Distracted by her call, Raphael snapped his head toward her direction. It was all the opportunity Felix needed to throw an uppercut, knocking Raphael backwards. Felix brought his burnt, deformed legs to his chest and barreled his clawed feet into Raphael's stomach, shooting Raphael up and into the ceiling. Raphael fell back to the ground bringing chunks of ceiling down with him. Felix scrambled out of the way. He saw the scroll on the desk. He dove for it, grabbing it with his remaining hand, and vaulted back through the hole in the ceiling and into the night sky.

Rachel rushed over to Raphael. "He took it! He took the scroll!"

Raphael tried to catch his breath. He looked at Rachel. "Are you all right?"

"No! I'm not all right! That disgusting animal just smashed into our office and took the document! What was that thing?!?"

"A fallen angel."

"A *WHAT!*" Rachel was stunned. "Raphael...what the hell is going on!?!"

Raphael thought hard and fast. "I need a copy of that scroll."

"I scanned it. It's on the computer."

Rachel moved toward the computer and brought the scanned document up onto the screen. Raphael quickly re-read its message. His eyes narrowed, "Gabriel's trumpet is no ordinary instrument. It heralds the seven plagues of Armageddon."

Rachel's face paled. "You mean the plagues mentioned in the *Book of Revelation?*"

"Yes, the very same. "

"And yet, you're sitting there, reading this without any hesitation, without pause..."

"Rachel, listen to me..."

"No, wait! *Wait*...you said the scroll was written in angelic language. Yet, somehow, *you* can read this." Rachel started to back away from him until she was at the opposite end of the office from where Raphael stood. Rachel could barely speak, "How? How can *you* possibly read this? You fought that thing. It knew your name!"

He lowered his chin so that his eyes bored into hers. "Think, Rachel. You already know the answer. I've already told you. I...*recognize*...*it*." Raphael moved toward her and grabbed her hands. "Hear me..."

She threw his hands off of her. As her breath quickened, panic set in as time slowed around her — the answer was there, colliding with all her reason, all her scientific study, all her human experience. She shook her head. "No...we're alone...they don't exist...they can't...that would mean...God *is* real..."

Raphael continued his laser beam stare that spoke directly to her mortal soul. "He always has been." He stepped slowly toward her and, as he did, he grew taller in height.

She tried to rationalize the tide of thoughts swirling in her head by speaking her thoughts aloud, "Only in scripture...only three were ever named. Michael...Gabriel...and..." She began to hyperventilate as Raphael grew even taller until he loomed over her at nine feet tall. He closed the distance between them. The last name breathed forth from her lips, *"Raphael..."*

Six sapphire wings jutted forth from his body extending the width of the room. "Yes, Rachel. I am the archangel Raphael, one of the seven who stand before the throne of God."

"Raphael...you...have...*wings*..." She barely whispered the words before she fainted. As Rachel fell to the floor, Raphael caught her in his massive arms. He looked down at her with disquietude. He moved her hair away from her pale face before turning his attention back onto Rachel's birthday present glowing on the computer screen. Raphael's eyes focused on one symbol and one symbol alone — the symbol for Gabriel. "Gabriel, what have you done?"

THE MESSENGER

Israel

"*You shall herald nothing, Gabriel. God's words will never be uttered from your mouth again.*"

Those were the last words Lucifer ever spoke to her — and then all went dark. Even now the stark memory of that moment haunted Gabriel to no end as she thought upon their last moment in heaven together. She was perched on top of a steeple in the Middle East. She was absolutely still. Her eyes were the only form of movement to her statuesque form. She had been crouched there for days as the war in the streets down below refused to die — watching, waiting. Her chestnut eyes missed nothing as the guns fired, as the bombs exploded, as the guilty cried, and as the innocent died. She watched it all — and did *absolutely nothing*.

Even as she witnessed the children in the street being slaughtered by the senseless warring that never ceased, she shed not a single tear. Her heart did not hammer in rage. Her spirit was not roused to justice. And at this very moment of earthly apathy, she realized this was not always so; *she* was not always so. There used to be laughter, there used to be joy; there used to be passion and fury brewing within the heart of God's greatest messenger. And it was all for the people, for God's created people. But all was still. All was quiet within the body of this archangel. And it was in the stillness that his voice haunted her in the reality of the play she watched down below.

"It is folly, Gabriel. And God knows this!"

A deep, heavy sigh escaped her as Lucifer's words filled her mind. Yes, God knew. God knew it was possible. God knew it the moment He gave them choice. He knew it the moment he gave them a playground called earth…that *this* was possible. And even worse…*Lucifer knew it was possible.* He himself had been the example of possibility — the irony of the past now the reality of the present as Gabriel looked upon the violence and chaos in the streets below. Infinite possibility made clear as humans exercised their mortal gift of free will.

Looking out at the painted picture of choice, Gabriel wondered, *Who chooses this? Who desires this?* Why speak of plagues that symbolize Armageddon when they were already here having been brought by human hand and human choice? Rivers had already turned red by humanity's constant slaughtering of one another; the sky had grown dark from pollution of an exhausted environment; fire rained down from all the explosions and bombs causing the trees and land to burn to the ground. Who needs revelations or the coming of an antichrist to turn a mother against a son when all you need is choice? *Too much choice.* And Gabriel had seen enough of unaccounted choice. In the pit of her stomach she knew what she did forty years ago was the right thing to do.

She slowly rose from the steeple having seen this play before.

Had there been a human being on the street that could see into the unseen world, they would have born witness to the knowledge that even an immortal can slowly die. Gabriel's wings, once a fiery scarlet red, were drooped and wilting. Their crimson color had lost their vibrancy. She looked withered, shrunken — barely the size of an average mortal as she rose from the steeple.

A bomb exploded in the building across the street from where Gabriel stood. She didn't even turn her head as the screams and cries began again. Unable to watch the next act in this twisted theater, she jumped from steeple to steeple, building to building, seeing the same scene on every street play out as the one before.

"They are not worthy of their creation, Gabriel. They would not understand their own likeness to our Father. To allow them to exist would be madness..."

Words he spoke before he ever laid eyes on them. Words he believed before their creation was certain. Words he spoke before he fell. Remembering them now, the thought came again...he was right. She had been sitting on that steeple for days knowing that he was. How long had she waited for a single human choice to show her he was wrong? How long? For years she had watched and seen nothing. And because of that, God's messenger had no heralds to bring but the last one, for God's messenger had nothing more to say. She was done talking. There was no one listening anyway...and she knew it.

Gabriel spread her six phoenix-like wings and launched into the sky. She soared higher and higher. Into the clouds she rose, out of the clouds she fell...until the cold wind came, *"Beloved..."*

Gabriel whirled around in midair at the sound of Lucifer's voice — not the haunted melody in her memory but a voice of the present. Forty years had passed since he called to her on the cold wind. Forty years since Gabriel buried a piece of herself in the desert. He was watching her then just as he has always watched her. The fact he spoke again to her now could only mean one thing...

Gabriel's eyes searched every direction for him, but there was nothing but white vapor and an eerie silence. And yet...she *felt* Lucifer's presence — waiting, watching. With barely a whisper she answered him, *"No."*

The cold wind blew against her face with the gentlest touch, *"My friend..."*

Gabriel moved away from the wind and dove down from the clouds away from him. She soared through the nighttime sky of the Western World and descended upon a desolate city. And just like the velvety dimness on a moonless night, every crack and crevice of this city was filled with darkness and shadow. No humans could be seen or heard, for the mortal souls who lived here had fallen asleep in their waking hour on this place called earth. Even with eyes wide open, they saw nothing. They searched for nothing. Justice was dead. Hope was gone. God was forgotten.

Yet, even in the darkness, Gabriel could see the malevolent shadows of the unseen world slithering across the landscape, for she knew them well — the demons of hell. The immortal fallen. Rebel warriors she once called friends. She could smell their rank odor — the smell of death and decay. She felt their venomous eyes on her rising up from the shadows below.

Gabriel continued on, flying softly across the lonesome region. Each building she passed she found abandoned, each block she traveled, no tree or flower grew; the streets themselves looked as if they had been fired upon ages ago, completely filled with smut and grime. But it was on these streets that the mirrors of her Father's face lived and breathed; it was on these streets that she heard their mortal grief, their pain, their numbness, their despair — and their groans were *everywhere*. The torment sounds loudest to the south of where she flew. It was to the south that Gabriel turned.

*   *   *

Gabriel landed silently on the poverty-stricken street having heard the lonely groans of the hookers and strung out junkies crowding it. Their cries of desperation rose and fell in the harmony of a somber song each one knew and each one shared; it was a song that mirrored the melody of their souls. It was a song only Gabriel could hear and she knew it well. It was the only one she has ever heard being sung — and it was sung in hell. To hear it on the earth was heartbreaking indeed — or, for Gabriel, it used to be.

Walking past the humans piled up on the street humming their sorrowful tune, Gabriel took in each and every one of their faces and thought only one thing: *These are the faces that were created in the image of the Most High God.* It was these very faces that she used to fight for against Lucifer's army of darkness. And it was these very faces that Gabriel had lost all empathy for. Seeing their wasted bodies and vapid looks on their faces, Gabriel knew this one thing: *the devil is winning his war.*

Gabriel walked on searching each and every one of their faces, listening with absolute focus for a single melody — a song of peace in a mortal soul. *There has to be one. There must be.* But there wasn't. And she walked on.

"They would live in darkness without God's light."

Lucifer's words filled her mind once again. It was then that she saw the growing movement on the shadows in the street. She could smell the sulfur and rank stench of burnt flesh. She could hear the shuffling of soot-filled wings and the scraping of feet and hands of her hunched and disfigured brethren. Gabriel could feel their hate-filled eyes watching her as she walked through their domain. She knew her presence on this street was like a blip on their radar pulling their attention toward her like a tractor beam as they crawled and slithered in the darkness — *and they were all coming.*

Gabriel continued to walk boldly down the street as the demons of the underworld scaled down from the buildings like cockroaches and rose up from the sewers like a flood of rats. Moloch, the leader of the fallen angels on the street, clung to the top of a lamppost. He leapt off of it and plunged down toward Gabriel. He swiped at her wilted wing with his clawed hand. He flew through the air past her, testing her. He rolled onto the ground behind her; his sword was drawn.

She stopped walking.

The fallen angel whirled back onto the sidewalk steeling himself for a battle with the archangel. But Gabriel did not turn. She walked on.

Not possible.

Moloch's blood-filled eyes narrowed in confusion. He pounded his fist into his chest and shouted at her with his gravelly voice, but no true word came out — only the caw of a murderous raven. His purposeful words had long left him since his fall from heaven. His sword was ready, but Gabriel didn't even bother to turn her head at his threatening cry.

Moloch looked at the other fallen angels around him unsure that what he saw before him was true. But they all had the same look on their distorted faces that he had — disbelief. Being so far from the light of God, Moloch had forgotten what it was like to live in the light, but there was one thing that Moloch had never forgotten: *Gabriel...always...fights.* She was an archangel. She was Michael's second-in-command. She was the only angel Lucifer ever confided in — his greatest friend in all of heaven. And the most important thing about Gabriel he never forgot: *she hated the demons of hell.*

Moloch still remembered that day in heaven when God formed the army. All the male angels battled it out with one another to earn their place. And then came Gabriel — small, unschooled, *and female.* The moment she stepped into the arena, no angel could have foreseen what was about to happen that day. To fight the archangel Michael? Insanity. No one could beat Michael. *No one.* But that didn't stop her. She lifted her sword and charged across the arena toward Michael. And she didn't just fight Michael to prove she was good enough to serve in God's army, she fought against Michael and almost beat him to lead it.

And here she was walking down their street filled with darkness. They felt her presence the moment she landed, having felt the vibration of her confident stride as she moved through their domain. Moloch and the other demons had moved in on her through the shadows in preparation for a long and arduous fight. They were ready. Standing on the sidewalk side by side staring at Gabriel with their weapons drawn, they still were.

As Moloch took in Gabriel's countenance, the only reaction his baiting caused was a single feather to fall from her wing. It was then that he was struck by Gabriel's changed appearance: her drooped wings, her shortened height, her tired gait and — *her lack of weapons.*

Moloch tensed and cackled a command that echoed across the

streets and darkened alleys. More demons poured onto the street in reply. Their warped garble rose in volume as they closed in on her, howling and jeering like a pack of hyenas as they did. Moloch clutched his sword in his clawed hand and raced toward Gabriel.

Like a silverback charging a challenger over his territory, he was almost upon her when Gabriel suddenly stopped walking and spun around. Moloch skidded to a halt on his knees, while the other demons scattered away from her and back onto the safety of their sidewalks and into the shadows of their alleys. Their voices were mollified as they cowered from her anticipated attack, for they knew they had provoked her into reckoning.

But Gabriel was not looking back at Moloch or any of the other demons. She was looking up at the midnight sky. Her eyes were wide as she searched it for something she alone had heard. A look of trepidation and anger collided onto her angelic face.

Without a word, Gabriel strode down the street toward Moloch, breaking into an all-out run. Defensively, Moloch crouched into attack position anticipating the impact of her blow. But before she smashed into him, she vaulted into the sky and was gone.

Moloch looked to her path in the sky in disbelief. He growled to himself, *"We find this…curious."*

The other demons trickled back onto the street looking in the direction Gabriel had flown. She was nowhere to be seen. The sky was starless.

And then it came…

A violent roar of thunder called out across the sky — a rumble unlike any sound the mortal world had ever heard before. And yet its monstrous cry *had* been heard before — heard by the fallen ones when all was light. Moloch's red eyes bulged in recognition. He spun around to the others and shouted a cry of warning.

"Creator! Punisher! Father!"

It was the sound of that thunder that brought about their chain of darkness. It was that rumble that broke the barrier from Heaven and hurled them into Hell. The demons scattered racing for the shadows and the darkness, for they knew the voice of the thunder — they knew the voice of God.

The crash of thunder was so deafening, that the humans covered their ears from the horrible booming sound. The hookers screamed in fear; the addicts were awakened from their drugged-out stupors. A turbulent wind swept through the streets causing all the hopeless souls unfortunate enough to be on it to run for cover, but there was no time to run — time had run out.

The thunder stopped and out of the clear dark sky came a rain of fire. It hammered down upon the street in a storm of fury, slamming into the buildings, cars and humans like gunfire. The street exploded in flames as the fire shot down upon it. The fire was utterly ruthless as its aim ripped through windows, pummeling everything in its path. Some of the humans on the street caught fire. Their screams were drowned out by the sound of the hardened rain barreling down upon them from above. Hiding in the shadows, the demons' red bulbous eyes watched in fear and amazement as the fire continued to demolish everything in sight — attacking everyone...*except for them.*

Moloch watched the fire fall all around him. He nervously extended his scarred hand to catch the flames, but the fire went right through his fingertips. He looked down at the flame on the street below. It was there that he saw it — *hail* — hail the color of Gabriel's wings; hail the color of blood. His eyes widened as he recognized this phenomenon; he recognized this plague.

A deep, throaty laugh rose up from his tar-colored lips. He jumped onto the street raising his deformed face to the sky. The rest of the demons watched as the fire left him unscathed as it rained down murderously upon him. Moloch's laughter rose as he lifted his arms wildly in the air.

"The kingdom...the kingdom..."

Watching their fellow demon as he swayed in jubilation, the rest of the fallen ones rolled onto the street feeding off of Moloch's wild, frantic energy. Moloch screeched a warped-sounding cry only a twisted mind could understand. In reply, the demons cawed like crows and exploded into a tribal-like, riotous rage. They smashed any remaining windows, tearing down the lampposts and telephone lines until turning their attention onto a group of humans.

They screamed their unheard cry as they approached the hookers and junkies, throwing the humans out from their shelter and onto the street by their unseen hands. The hail slammed down upon them immediately brutalized the humans. They tried to run back to their shelters but were trapped by the demons' unseen arms. The demons bounced the humans around as if it were a game. Their razor-sharp teeth gleamed as they watched the humans catch fire, drooling at the sight of the mortal bodies burning alive. And as the men and women were devoured in flame…the demons danced; they danced like jungle monkeys, for the time had come when the earth would be consumed by fire and death — closely resembling their palace in hell.

Moloch looked on his fellow angels as they moved to the beat of their own drum, dancing around the mound of fire that was once human flesh. Seeing their burnt lips pulled back in ugly sneers of glee, he thought of how different this sight before him was than the one when they were first cast into the heart of the inferno. There was pain and terror then. There was despair. There was death. And even amongst the echo of defeat, there was hope...and it was there in hell where the light at the end of their tunnel had finally come...and his name was *Lucifer*.

I, LUCIFER

After the Fall from Heaven

Hell was thought to have been a myth — a place that could not possibly exist. For what could be the purpose of such a despicable, unlivable, vile place as the domain called *hell?* To have a place so utterly opposite of the paradise of the seven heavens, it *had* to be myth, for God always had a purpose for everything he did, everything he created, everything he willed. *But a fire world?* What reason could there possibly be for such a place? No angel in heaven ever knew. No angel had ever actually seen the realm that burned eternally and rained nothing but sulfur and ash. No angel could even remember how they had even heard of the inferno. But as the former chief seraphim in all of heaven stood on its banks, the realization that such a place existed and that it was meant for him, was more than he could bear.

"*Lucifer...*"

He did not turn at the sound of his name. Lucifer did not even offer a blink of recognition behind his ice blue eyes. He continued to stare out at the lava waves of the Lake of Fire that mocked his despair, rolling on top of themselves, beckoning to him like a longtime lover, whispering him toward his immortal death. His golden hair once glistening in the light of God's sun was covered in ash. The blackened soot and sands of this burnt-out lair now tarnished his armor so noble in battle. The pentagram of the Morning Star etched on his breastplate had faded to gray.

To have known him before this moment was to know the beauty of God. It was to glimpse the full breath of your entirety — that all things were connected in you and you in them. Lo, to behold the depth that God and the angel Lucifer loved one another was like the sun shining down upon the lilies in the field. The beauty of God's creation illuminated by the light; the lily beckoning and absorbing the rays of the sun so that the two became one — a thread of giver and receiver linked by the desire to give life and live.

To know that the lily would fold its petals upon itself and turn away from the sun so willingly — believing that it rose higher than the sun and no longer needed it; thinking it could draw upon itself for sustenance and revolt against what nature intended was...*ludicrous. Folly.* For what flower could live without the sun?

But, alas, Lucifer was that lily. He desired nothing more than to shed his petals and became the sun itself. And so he gathered unto himself more lilies. Breathing words of independence and self-righteousness that they, too, would turn away from the sun of their making and extend their petals to the light of an artificial one. And many, too many, turned from the sun of the Father's light and toward a false light that rose like the dawn — that of the Morning Star — that of Lucifer.

"Lucifer!"

Beelzebub called to him again, yet Lucifer could not will himself to turn from this mythical reality to the one that awaited behind him. So unbelievable — that God could do this...to *him.* Lucifer stood there — immobile, paralyzed — so statue-like and lifeless was his form that only the slight rise and fall of his chest gave any evidence that Lucifer was still amongst the living.

They had almost won. They had fought against Michael and his remaining army — an army that no longer held the best warriors in it,

43

for they had joined Lucifer's side. Victory was certain. Triumph was inevitable. They were within mere yards of the kingdom's sapphire steps that led to the throne. God would have been overthrown and the abomination his father had created would have been destroyed by now. Lucifer would have control of heaven. Lucifer alone would reign.

But it all went wrong.

Out of nowhere, the archangels had surrounded his army and trapped them. Archangels that never should have been there. Archangels that had been methodically removed from the battle's plain. *But they were all there!*

And then from the sky…she came. She came with her fury and her pain and her rage — and she directed it down upon him.

Gabriel.

He himself had made certain that she would never be anywhere ever again. But there she was — a newly resurrected phoenix — and she was aiming her lightning bolt at him. *Not possible.* He had never seen her coming.

"Lucifer…we are undone."

Undone.

Hearing the pleading tone in Beelzebub's voice, he still could not will himself to turn. Not yet.

"Thousands have perished in the fall. Many of our brethren are injured; they've been severely burnt by the flames and heat of this place. They're disfigured." Beelzebub paused, lifting his head to his leader. "I need to give them direction and counsel, but I have none to give."

Perished.

"Whispers are rising over another battle, another war."

Beelzebub dropped his cherubic head of pale hair in exhaustion and despair. The cherub's heart weighed heavily as he tried to contain his emotions over their punishment and defeat. *"Answer me…"*

His anger rising, Beelzebub beseeched his leader once more, *"Lucifer…"*

Silence.

Lucifer continued his frozen stare at the Lake of Fire. Beelzebub noticed that his eyes held the look of a lost child. He had been standing before this lake for days now, watching its malevolent current swallow his fellow angels whole. And yet, they kept falling — falling from heaven, falling into the lava waves' pull and wake — perishing once and for all. What was immortal now made mortal.

The lake itself was massive, stretching from the brimstone bank where Lucifer stood to the valley of razor-sharp onyx mountains stretching miles behind it. Its heat was too intolerable to bear — so suffocating was its stench, so endless its reach. The glow of the orange-hot lava flickered across Lucifer's eyes.

Staring helplessly at his chief, Beelzebub had no other choice but to turn away from him and toward the throng of surviving angels in order to comfort them himself, but he too was in need of comfort. And the one who could give it would not stir. Failing to rouse the greatest angel in all of heaven, and seeing that he too was as lost as the rest of them, Beelzebub suddenly understood what it was to feel despair.

What were they to do now?

God had thrown them out of Heaven so violently that they couldn't fight against the force of his hand as they were rocketed down into Hell. That out-of-control flight as he fell from heaven was so terrifying, Beelzebub had no idea if his body would ever stop its spiraling free fall. The moment he plummeted into the hard ground, seeing the fire and brimstone storming all around him, he couldn't believe what he was seeing. *The inferno.* The myth. *Hell.* What was one to think now that they were in it? How was one to live now that they were here? How was one…*to get back home?*

With a heavy heart, he turned and faced his fellow brethren. Staring into their ashen-gray faces, their burnt wings, their distorted scarred flesh, their lifeless stares and tears, he was as lost as the survivors he was seeking to guide. *Their faces…*so different from when they were in the light. Angels whose hearts were filled with such passion, such grace, such desire to be more than what they were told to be, now only phantoms of their former selves as they sat on the ashen sands of perdition.

He looked to Gokor.

Seeing the powerful cherub sitting on the blackened boulder, holding onto his severed wings with a look of shock was one Beelzebub never thought possible. Lilith, a female cherub, sobbed silently at his feet. Looking at the army before him, all he saw were a sea of faces: faces of the lost, faces of the fearful, faces filled with woe. He turned away from Gokor, feeling a deep sob rising up from within. Trying to hold it in, he looked out at the Gate of Hell. Even from where he stood, he could see its welcome engraved on the door. He could see the body parts of falling angels piling up around its base. *Death*. Looking at their lifeless faces, Beelzebub was hit with the realization that he was not the leader of this army he thought he was.

Michael was the one who led. Michael was the one who always knew what to do. He was the one who trained them. He was the one Beelzebub wished to be like, and yet Michael was the one they had all betrayed. *And for what?* All Beelzebub wanted was a chance — a chance to show that he too could lead. And it was at this very moment, standing between a sea of woe and a lake of death, that Beelzebub suddenly realized that you should always be wary of what you wish for...you just may get it.

Beelzebub lowered his head in grief. *There was an enemy in heaven*, Michael said. That's how it all began. *An enemy*...How that knowledge infuriated Beelzebub like no other. How dare such a creature roam the beauty of the heavens, free and unclaimed, bringing shadow to the magnificence of his home. He abhorred it. He despised it. How he wanted to hunt the enemy down. But who it was, Michael would not say. But Michael knew. Beelzebub could see it behind Michael's eyes. Of course, Michael knew.

And so they waited.

Beelzebub and the rest of the army were on high alert, ready for Michael's orders to take the angel down. How he wished to be the one to find him; the one to chain such a foul creature who prided himself on bringing darkness to his home in heaven. And he wasn't the only one. They all wanted justice; they all wanted to bring this angel before the Host to be tried before the Principalities. Why God allowed the enemy to roam freely, the angels never knew. Yet Michael seemed to have the answer. *"God is waiting. He is allowing the enemy time to see if he will continue on the path he has chosen or seek that of righteousness once again."*

It made sense. God had given them free will. And no one knew what the enemy had done or what he was about to do, but if an angel were an enemy, that would mean…he had turned away from God.

Beelzebub looked up at Lucifer. Little did any of them know that the enemy…*was he. He lied to us! Deceived us!* He looked out at the Lake of Fire and watched more of his fellow brethren drowning amongst the lava waves. They reached out to him, to Lucifer, to all of them, but there was nothing they could do. Seeing their hands as they sank amongst the molten rock, Beelzebub's anger rose. He could bear it no longer. He shifted his eyes to Lucifer and pulled his sword from his sheath. *If we must suffer for this betrayal, so must he!*

Beelzebub advanced toward his chief. *His fault…his fault…his…*He was almost upon him when Lucifer suddenly spoke, "I am going to tell you a story…"

Beelzebub stopped dead in his tracks. Lucifer's voice was so faint he wasn't even sure he heard it. But when he saw the heads of the fallen army rise up, he knew that his commander had finally awakened. For Lucifer's voice was the sound their ears burned to hear — for his was the voice that could yield a command like a mighty sword; his was the voice that resounded strength as it ordered the thunder and lightning in heaven, his was the voice that ignited the fire in their hearts to pick up their swords to follow him and fight. It was the voice that led them to the steps of God's kingdom…*and straight into Hell.* For it was the voice…*that lied.*

And now that voice had changed. Gone was the strength and confidence that once filled it, for Lucifer's melodious voice now carried the tune of sorrow. Beelzebub was thrown by the sound of his vulnerability. He slowly lowered his weapon.

"It is the story of a father and his son." Lucifer's voice wavered. "This son loved his father with all his heart, for his father was everything to him — *utter perfection*. And the son yearned for that perfection, for in it was his father's love, his father's thoughts, his father's counsel and confidence. And the son did everything his father commanded him, leaning on all the knowledge his father had to give. And all that he did was good in the eyes of his father, for the father loved his son."

Tears streamed down his unblinking eyes.

"And so the son grew to be more like the father in all ways. He strived to be the mirror of him so that the father's face would shine upon him. And the son lived for those moments — the moments of intimacy and praise, for his heart thundered in anticipation of what more he could do bring the light down upon him. And all was well..."

The angels listened on in silence, never before having been invited into Lucifer's mind, for it was a mind he shared with no angel, save one — and *she* had abandoned him. Lucifer watched the fire rain down before his pale blue eyes. He caught an ignited piece of ash in the palm of his hand.

"And then one day the father told the son his *own* story — so horrific, so vile, so unbelievable that the son knew it must be pretend. But the father was the essence of truth, and so the son listened closer to understand his father's words. And words they were indeed. Words that were tainted; words that were flawed, for the words the father spoke were no mere story — they were words that were true."

Lucifer closed his hand around the fiery piece of ash, clenching it in his powerful fist. He looked out at the tar-colored sky above. "The story was to become reality and the father sought to do it with all his power and all his might. But the son saw what the father did not — that the father's story should never have been written. That its words should never have been thought. And for the first time, they quarreled. They fought. And the son was in agony, for the father would not listen! He would not hear! And the father turned his son away. He turned him out of his home." Lucifer's body shook. "The son was betrayed by his father. And the son...the son was...*heartbroken.*"

Lucifer lowered his head and...*wept*. His cries were so devastating, so filled with anguish that some of the angels turned away. His body racked in grief as the waves of sorrow washed over his shattered heart grieving for all that was, all that is, and all that would never be again. *"THE FATHER IS NOT PERFECT!!!"*

Lucifer's pained voice roared across the valley of onyx-colored mountains.

Gone were the white cliffs of heaven he soared over for thousands of years. Gone was heaven's ever-changing sky exchanged with one polluted by brimstone. Gone was the music...*the music...the music* — the true sound of his voice. Lucifer's eyes were wild with rage as the images of his home, his paradise now lost flashed across his mind. He clenched his fists. His body trembled as he looked up at the blackened sky.

"THE FATHER IS FALSE IN THE EYES OF HIS SON!!! CREATOR GOD! MOCKER OF LIFE AND OF BEAUTY! THE SON, TOO, HAS EYES!!!" He cried out to the sulfur raining down from above. "YOU HAVE WRONGED YOUR SON! HERE IN THIS PLACE FROM HELL AND BACK I WILL RIGHT YOU! YOU CANNOT TURN OUT YOUR CREATION LIKE A FORGOTTEN DREAM! YOU CANNOT TAKE YOUR FACE FROM ME! WE ALL MUST ANSWER FOR WHAT WE'VE DONE! *EVEN YOU!!!*" His fury vibrated across the realm of perdition. "I KNOW WHAT IT IS YOU DO! AND IT IS WRONG IN THE EYES OF YOUR SON!!!"

Breathless, Lucifer lowered his head. He slowed his breathing and whispered the words of his tormented heart, *"You will hear me...I will make you hear me..."*

Lucifer turned to face the surviving angels. He advanced on Beelzebub. Beelzebub tried to back away, but Lucifer closed the distance with determined steps. The look on his face was lethal. He grabbed Beelzebub by the throat. Lifting him up, Beelzebub tried to fight him off. Lucifer ripped Beelzebub's sword from his hand and angled it at one of Beelzebub's eyes. He moved the blade closer.

"Do you not see, Beelzebub? We are not undone. We have merely *fallen*." He kept the tip right at Beelzebub's pupil; the look in Lucifer's eye was one of pure fury. *"I...see...you..."*

He dropped Beelzebub and strode toward the rebel army. He hurled Beelzebub's sword into the Lake of Fire. It dissolved the moment it hits the fiery waves.

Lucifer surveyed the remaining army. Their eyes were all on him as he took in their countenance, for this was the army that stormed heaven's kingdom to its very footsteps. This was the army that held the brightest and noblest hearts and minds to ever traverse heavens' grounds — Powers, Thrones, Dominions. This was the army that remained loyal to him in an argument he had with God that they knew nothing about. This was the army that sought independence alone, for that was what their hearts rioted for: liberation to grow beyond the close watch of their Father. Looking upon their shattered faces, Lucifer was not saddened nor angered, but comforted — for they were with him still. And for that, he would raise this army up once again.

"Brothers! Hear me! For I will tell you our father's story of horror...the story of why we have truly fallen from grace."

Beelzebub's eyes narrowed in confusion.

"The Father told me of a grand plan he had in the making — the greatest experiment of his heart. 'Behold, Lucifer, I will make another creature — one designed in my own image. A breed very like an angel, but one made of dust and bone.'" He let this settle in. "A plan that, in the eyes of the son, was unnatural and grotesque — *folly*."

The angels were bewildered.

"But what the Father did not tell was that it was not just an idea, but that it had already been done."

Angels rose from the ground in fear and shock.

"Angels, our Father has done the unthinkable. He has experimented with the great divide and made what was immortal — *mortal*."

Gokor and other angels rose up in response, "Weaker beings of less design! Why would our Father do this?"

Nero, a Herculean Dominion, shouted, "You said 'they.' What does this mean?"

"There is more than one; how many I do not know, but of male and female nature they have come."

Vitor, a Cherub with emerald-colored eyes, slowly moved toward Lucifer. "What is this you speak of! I saw no such creature of newness or genesis in the heavens!"

"Nor did I, Vitor. Nor would any of you. They are not *in* the heavens."

There was stirring amongst the army at Lucifer's words. Nero continued to shout, "If they are not in the heavens, where else would they be!"

The angels waited on Lucifer's words, breathless and trembling at the knowledge he had yet to reveal. Beelzebub slowly stood and closed in on Lucifer, studying him.

Seeing their eyes on him, Lucifer knew he had them once again. "God has created a place of paradise — almost identical to heaven and yet not. This paradise can be destroyed as the creatures can be destroyed — for it, too, is mortal. He has given this paradise to his new creatures and placed them there. Our Father calls this place 'Earth' and the creatures…he calls *mankind*."

The angels were beside themselves. "But why! What is the point of this? Are we not enough for God!" The shout came from the Virtue — Azriel.

"No…*we're not*."

The angels were stunned.

"Why would we ever think we alone were enough for Him? Our father is a creator of worlds. That is what He loves. He grows and expands, an unstoppable force of energy without a point of original momentum. He simply is. He simply does. And the point...that mankind should live and return to heaven to finally see their Maker's face."

More angels were angered at his words. Gokor's face was grave. "How? How if they are flawed in design? How, if they are mortal?"

Lucifer looked him dead in the eye. "Our Father has breathed pieces of himself into their bodies. He has given them *souls*."

Azriel trembled, "Lucifer...I do not understand this. If they have souls, He has given them an even greater gift. He has raised them higher than us angels."

"Yes, Azriel, he has. God divided us up into the hierarchy so that our talents would best suit the needs of these creatures — to help them live well in the eyes of our father, to serve them and protect them when there was a need."

Lucifer walked amongst the army.

"*SLAVES!* WE ARE THE GREATEST WARRIORS HEAVEN HAS EVER SEEN! And we were to be slaves forever!" His eyes were ablaze. "*Insult!* For the Father has done something more unthinkable...he's given these beings the ability to procreate."

Nero could stand it no longer. "He gave them the power of creation! But only God creates!"

"*Not anymore.*"

Nero shook his head in disbelief, "Why didn't you tell us? Had more angels shared this knowledge, there would have been more to join our side. For I know no angel that would hear this news and be comforted by it. They would have rebelled against it."

Angels shouted in agreement. "Perhaps I should have. But I believed that revealing this knowledge to the angelic host would have given birth to fear. Fear leads to anger and a weakening of reason. Uncontrollable action breeds defensive emotion, and chaos would have erupted in the offense. Fighting has never been a means to an end in my mind, but I knew a skilled army with God's greatest soldiers would have kept order in the light.

"So I sought an alternate means to recruit you all by offering you a means to seek that which you stormed the kingdom for — freedom and independence! You all sought it with or without this knowledge. And with God overthrown, order through my reign yielded by you would have been done! We all would have had what we wanted!"

Gokor spoke, "And that is why you fought with God that day when Michael found you unconscious on the steps of the kingdom."

"Yes, Gokor. I told God it was madness to put this plan into action. And for that alone, He turned his face from me. A son should always be allowed to ask questions, for isn't that what children often do? And the Father should always answer — especially when he alone has them. But He would not bend! He had to be stopped from damning us into slavery by his misguided will! I beg your understanding in my plight. I did not wish to deceive you nor did I wish to bring madness to our paradise. My only intent was to keep order whilst overthrowing the madness of our Father!"

All was silent on hell's grounds. Moments went by before anyone spoke. "They must die."

Lucifer looked to the angel who had spoken the words — it was Asmodeus. Angels whispered their agreement and disagreement, but all the while Asmodeus and Lucifer held each other's stare — a mutual understanding passed between the two. Asmodeus continued, "If mankind is as you say, then they do not deserve to live. They are an abomination — mutations of us. They have tainted the celestial line. It is up to us to keep it pure if God refuses to see!"

He moved between Gokor and Lucifer. "We abort the creation. We fire the earth and burn it down."

Azriel now stood. "Yes, kill it all."

Felix shouted, "No! Kill the creatures, but let the earth live! If you say that this place is likened to heaven, then let us live there. It would far better suit us than this place of filth and stench!"

Agreement was heard amongst the angels. Beelzebub continued to take in all the arguments and answers from the rebel army. His eyes, however, never left Lucifer's face.

Gokor's mighty voice shouted amongst the voices, *"Silence!"* He turned to the army. *"Heaven* is our home! I do not wish to reside in a dimension that lies less than the design of heaven! If God is so willing to give mankind a place of independence away from the light — our very own desire — then we riot against it. We continue to lay our fight at God's door! God must answer for this! He must answer to us! We have always done good in the eyes of our Father! Even in our rebellion, we have been misunderstood. Is this not a reason to fight to live where we rightfully belong?"

Vitor argued, "Another battle? Look at us! We are not ready for another fight. We are left here in this place of hell! And we *are* left, make no mistake! Had God wanted us to be liberated, he would have banished us to his earth! He will never allow us to touch it! Here is where we have been thrown! Here is where we are to remain until God allows us back in to heaven!"

Some angels murmured their agreement. Vitor continued on, "But to fire upon the earth, a place we have never seen — to destroy creatures we have yet to lay eyes on so that we may rule there and live there is madness! We do not know what these creatures are capable of. Would they not fight for their home just as we have done and still seek to do? Surely, they will fight!"

Nero turned to Vitor, *"You* are the one who is mad to think that we will remain here in a place so unlike the paradise we call home! We must go to the earth!"

Vitor stepped to Nero, "Am I mad? Our paradise is lost, Nero. Even I can barely bear the weight of this judgment that has been branded us as rebels and enemies of our Father. No matter what we have done, we can undo it. *This* is what our Father has dealt us for joining an army whose sole objective was to overthrow him. Is this not punishment we deserve?"

Azriel chimed in, "He is right. God threw us out. He has rid us from his sight. He will never let us back in. That blackened gate above us is a sign of our banishment into this prison. Even if we could fly to heaven, Michael will have everyone on armed watch. Uriel and the rest of the army will be guarding Heaven's Gate.

Heaven is no longer our home. It is not even an option in the immediate present. We are not ready for another battle — not yet. Here is where we must stay to rebuild our army. Earth and its creatures can wait."

Gokor replied, "I did not choose to rebel against my Father with hell in the equation. Even with the odds against us, fighting is the only way back in to heaven. That is my rightful home! I am ready!"

Vitor sighed deeply. "But I am not. Perhaps, we seek peace. We seek…forgiveness. We beg for God's mercy. Then we would not have to fight."

Lucifer raised an eyebrow. "*Forgiveness?* Forgiveness because you are sorry for bringing shadow to the light, or forgiveness because you are sorry you are here?"

Vitor remained silent.

"Even if you ask for forgiveness, Vitor, would you be satisfied going back to the kingdom to be an angel chained in slavery knowing what you know now? Or…do you stay here to embrace the angel that you can become?" He looked out at the army surrounding him, "For I believe hell is a place of opportunity. A place where our greatness can shine unlike any light we ever held before."

Azriel weighed Lucifer's words. "So you think that we should rebuild here."

Lucifer's eyes narrowed. "Not just rebuild here…*rule* here."

The angels erupted. Nero was seething, "*NO!* IT IS TO THE EARTH WE MUST GO! IT IS THE EARTH THAT WILL SET US FREE!"

Gokor erupted, "HEAVEN! IT IS HEAVEN THAT IS OURS!"

Lucifer shouted to the army, "HEAR ME, BROTHERS!" The angels' voices died down. "We shook the throne, my friends! Heaven is not lost to us! We *are* free! God in his banishment has severed all ties. We *are* liberated. He is not here. He is also…not on the earth."

The angels breathed in his words, pondering them.

"My friends, always remember: there are *other* ways of accomplishing one's goal. When one door closes, another one opens.

There is always another way to regain all that we have lost..."

Gokor scoffed, "It is either a battle in Heaven, prison in Hell or dwelling upon the Earth."

Lucifer turned his ice-cold eyes to Gokor, "That is where you have to broaden your mind, Gokor, for the game has changed. There are more players in the mix; there are more domains. It is to the players we must go."

The angels were silent once again. Lucifer continued, "I have listened to your arguments, and now you will hear mine. For I have stood on the banks of hell and pondered the way back to the light. The way to win is to find our opponent's strength *and* his weakness. And then we take it apart piece by piece. We know God's strength, but we forgot about his weakness."

Beelzebub finally decided to speak, "God has no weakness, Lucifer."

"Oh, but He does...he *loves*."

A faint smile formed on Lucifer's lips.

"We are the greatest angels amongst the Seraphim, Cherubim, Thrones, Powers. We are the greatest warriors heaven has ever seen! To be weak is to be miserable. Ambition...that we have. Power...we will obtain. We *shall* remain here and build ourselves a kingdom of our own! A house of pain that echoes the injustice of our very own hearts, but it shall not be a kingdom built for us, but a prison for all those who will help us in our goal to bring justice to the light." Lucifer looked at Gokor, "Another war will be waged, but that war will not be in heaven."

A faint smile curled on the corner of Gokor's lips. The fallen ones listened ever closer to the leader amongst them. "It will be a war greater than any other war that has come before. It will be a tidal wave of pain seven times greater than the insult we have been dealt by being cast down into the shadows of this place."

Asmodeus shouted, "If not a war in heaven, then *where*?"

Lucifer lowered his voice that all may hear and pay attention, "It is on the earth that the war will be waged. The Father has a weakness, my friends, oh yes — his unconditional love for all his creation. His love would then include mankind and his earth. So I tell you, we shall come upon these creatures called Men. We shall study them and find where their weakness lies."

Vitor interrupted him, "God will not allow you to corrupt his creation. Michael and Gabriel…"

At the sound of Gabriel's name, Lucifer whirled around and grabbed hold of Vitor.

"No, God won't allow it. He will be forced to come down from heaven and face us once again."

Vitor held Lucifer's stare. He looked deep into Lucifer's ice-blue eyes. His voice was barely a whisper, "She knew, didn't she? That is why Gabriel did not choose to stand with you."

Lucifer's jaw clenched; his eyes glowed in absolute fury. "You want forgiveness, Vitor? Ask him then. Make your amends with God and beg for his mercy, for you will not find his mercy here. There is no word I have spoken here or in heaven that you have not wanted to hear. You call them lies, but I only know truth — and my truth has set us free. But you do not want to hear my kind of truth." He released him. "Go then. Seek God amongst the solace of the shadows here in hell. No one will stop you."

Vitor looked upon his band of brothers. He turned toward the fallen angels, his fellow soldiers, his friends of old. Not a single one met his eye. Vitor turned to a redheaded angel, "Moloch?"

Moloch lowered his head. Remorse spread across Vitor's face in the knowing that every remaining angel here would meet his doom far beyond the borders of this place. The earth would never be theirs to rule, for they had yet to realize that even if they didn't want to serve, God had commanded the remaining angels in heaven to do it — and they would. The angels would fight for the humans and with the humans to defend the light of God's creation against the rebel angels of hell. He knew not the nature of mankind, but if they had been created in the image of his Father, just as the angels had been, they would not be easily destroyed. They would weigh the justice of their hearts and choices just as the angels had done. Another war would come, and just like the one that had just taken place, rebels against God would not win. They would never win. And the insanity of it all was that no one believed that God would hold them accountable for any of it — even now, these angels he had called his friends, his family — did not see that they would still be held accountable. Hell was merely purgatory for what awaited them in the end.

Vitor turned away from the army and walked toward the blackened mountains of hell.

"Let Vitor go, my friends, and think not on him again. He has chosen his own path. And I choose to stand with you on the one you now choose, for it is a path of light burning for us in the darkness."

Nero thundered, "Then it is to the earth we go!" He extended his hand to Gokor, "What say you, brother!"

Gokor grabbed onto Nero's hand. Gokor lifted one of his severed wings into the air, *"TO THE EARTH!!!"*

Like a tsunami, the rebel army rose up, lifting their weapons to the ashen sky as they chanted, *"EARTH! EARTH! EARTH!"*

Lucifer shouted amongst the throng, "I, too, shall go with you, my friends!" He looked into the eyes of all the angels. "Not to seek power for myself, but to stand with you, for I am a servant unto you alone, my brothers! My counsel in Heaven shall extend here in Hell! For I would rather reign here with you than serve in heaven! And when heaven is ours once again, we shall rule and reign together, for this story has not ended but is only beginning! *The Father will see his sons again!"*

Nero, Azriel, Gokor and Asmodeus chanted Lucifer's name until all of hell was filled with the sound of it. *"LUCIFER! LUCIFER! LUCIFER!"*

The only angel that remained silent was Beelzebub.

Lucifer humbly bowed before them. He slowly stood and looked out at the army surrounding him. A glimmer of satisfaction shone brilliantly behind his cerulean eyes as he looked upon their faces. *Yes, they are with him still.*

As he scanned the sea of face before him, he lifted his eyes to the blackened mountains beyond. It was then he saw her — *Gabriel.*

The archangel stood boldly on the mountaintop across from him, her six scarlet wings were spread wide.

His body stiffened; his eyes grew wide in the realization: *she has heard, she has heard, she has heard it all.*

Beelzebub caught his look. He followed Lucifer's gaze and saw Gabriel. He slowly looked back at Lucifer. His eyes narrowed as he studied the enemy's face. *Gabriel…she knew…and yet she did not stand beside him. The enemy…with all that he has revealed, what has he not said?*

A portal opened above Gabriel.

Lucifer, breathless, watched her rise up to the light; their eyes never left one another as she silently took flight back into heaven.

AWAKE

Oxford University

"**R**achel."

Rachel opened her eyes at the sound of Raphael's voice. She could barely make out the fuzzy outline of his enormous frame as he hovered over her. She continued to concentrate on his face until her blurred vision became clear and his silver eyes came into focus. "I just fainted, didn't I?"

Raphael nodded. He gently helped her sit up. "I always wondered what it would feel like to faint. I just never thought it would be because...wait, what happened?"

She looked at Raphael looming over her at his bursting height of over nine-feet-tall. His wings had retracted, but his towering form had yet to shrink back into its former human self. The memory of the events that occurred leading up to her dazed body lying on the floor came rushing back. "Oh yes, now I remember. I was just stating the fact that angels don't exist and you suddenly grew three feet and sprouted wings. Happy birthday to me."

"I'm an archangel." Raphael crossed his muscular arms over his broad chest. "We're no mere guardians of mankind, Rachel. We are warriors for God."

Rachel stared at him, taking in his enlarged body and its peacock-colored wings. With the absence of his glasses, she noticed the deep color of his gray eyes as if she was seeing them for the very first time; they were unlike any shade of gray she had ever seen. For a split second Rachel wondered how she never noticed their strange color before. She wondered how many other signs she had missed every day of her waking life. *Have I been sleeping the entire time?* But now her eyes were open and she *saw* all of Raphael. Taking in his perfectly carved body and utterly strange, yet beautiful face, and those eyes…

"Rachel, say something."

She snapped out of her daze. "You must forgive me, Raphael. I'm still in shock. This has been quite a day for me and I'm a bit overwhelmed, you see. I had no idea that my best friend wasn't human; that things that I didn't believe…exist whether I believed them or not, and that the things that I depended on knowing are no longer real. It's almost as if the mirror has cracked for me — and I don't know if I feel freed by it, betrayed, or preferred to be back in the realm of ignorance. I have yet to catch up to this moment."

She slowly stood, trying to gauge her bearings and collect her thoughts. Seeing his glasses lying on the desk, Rachel turned to him, "Why are you here with me? Why have you been here with me for four years pretending to be a linguistics professor when you're an angel??

"*Arch*angel."

"*ARCHANGEL!*" She grunted in utter frustration. She breathed deeply before continuing, "Why bother with *me*? This doesn't make sense, Raphael."

"God, my father, gave me an assignment — *you*. He commanded that I come to earth to protect you."

"From what?"

"I didn't know at the time. But I was told never leave your side, only revealing myself in true form when I felt it necessary."

"But why me?"

Raphael lowered his arms and looked at the document Rachel's father sent. "I believe the answer lies in this. Your father's intentions for sending this to you have troubled me greatly, but it's this piece of paper that has made it clear to me why I've been sent."

Looking at the symbols, Raphael's translation rang in her ears. "What does it all mean, Raphael? Gabriel and his trumpet…"

"*Her* trumpet."

Rachel did a double take. "Gabriel is *female?*"

"Yes, and a very terrifying one when she wants to be. That's why she has to start all her messages off with 'Fear not' and 'Do not be afraid.' But, um…don't tell her I said that, okay?"

She did not answer.

Raphael panicked. "Rachel, *please???*"

"Why does everyone think she's male?"

"If you were a man, would you admit when you were scared to death by a female archangel so that it could be recorded for all eternity to read about? The men of that time were extremely prideful."

"I see your point. So why did she bury it?"

"I don't know what would possess Gabriel to bury her trumpet that has the power to call to the Four Winds and end this world, but she must have had her reasons — and I trust them."

Rachel did not seem convinced. "Do you?"

"Yes, I do. I've always trusted her." Raphael looked away. "Something must have compelled her to do it when the antichrist was born. That's the only clue the document reveals."

"The antichrist…is my father the antichrist?"

Raphael looked at her aghast. "No! Your father's part in this has yet to be revealed, but know that he is not it."

Rachel relaxed. She was slowly piecing the puzzle together. "So Gabriel buries the trumpet when the antichrist is born. And then she writes about, letting anyone who comes across it know that she did so, leaving it for anyone to find."

"This is not her writing."

"Then…whose is it?"

Raphael's eyes turned cold. "Satan's." He pointed to the

pentagram at the bottom of the first page. A chill ran down her spine as her eyes rested upon the signature.

Rachel slowly backed away from the desk. She rubbed her hands up and down her arms to warm herself. "What kind of angel is Gabriel?"

"What do you mean?"

"Whose side is she on?"

"The good side."

"I don't believe you."

Raphael turned toward Rachel, his face was severe. "I never lie, Rachel! Gabriel despises Satan and all who follow him — angels and humans alike."

"Then how would the devil know she buried it if they were not in league with one another? You yourself said you don't know why she buried the trumpet. How do you know she didn't do it to join his side?"

"My heart tells me it isn't so. Gabriel is God's messenger, Rachel. Satan pays particular attention to her actions in order to know the will of God. He watches her — *always*. Her missions carry the messages of Heaven on her wings to the people of the Earth — prophecies and plans of my Father that shift the course of humanity by offering them choices of their will. She has never shared those messages with the devil! *Not ever!*"

He paused, lost in the memories of the past, reminded of Gabriel and Lucifer and how they once were together — until the darker memory came, casting its shadow over the brighter one devouring it whole. He closed his eyes to keep that memory away, but he could not block it out. *No…she would never…not after what he did…*

"What is it, Raphael?"

Raphael saw the vision of a moment long past in his mind — one that he had never spoken of before. "Before the Rebellion in Heaven, Gabriel and Lucifer were inseparable, the best of friends. How they loved one another…it was before the celestial hierarchy was created and we angels were named to different divisions — given a clearer vision of the purpose of our creation. Seraphim. Cherubim. Thrones. Dominions. Principalities. Powers. Virtues. Angels and Archangels. It was then that everything changed. Lucifer was the head of the hierarchy, Chief Seraph — our leader. And he was mesmerizing, Rachel — how we all loved him but Gabriel most of all. Lucifer stood closest to God breathing our father's thoughts down to the rest of the hierarchy starting with him. That is when it all changed. That is when the shadows came to drown out my Father's light.

"Lucifer had recruited an army of my brothers and sisters to fight at his side in a lunatic attempt to overthrow God and seize the kingdom of heaven for his own. The rebel angels he recruited were the best warriors of God's army — the army Michael commanded. Lucifer had recruited one-third of the entire angelic host — something so unfathomable, Rachel, that I still cannot comprehend how easily it had been done. He tried to recruit Gabriel thinking that she, of all angels, would stand beside him."

Raphael looked at Rachel; distress blanketed itself across his face, for he remembered. "She refused."

Tears stung his pale gray eyes. "Gabriel did not extend her hand to help him in his war with God. And Lucifer's reaction…" He shook his head in anger. He looked her dead in the eye, "She's on the good side, Rachel."

Rachel absorbed the pained expression on Raphael's face. "I know what it's like to love a man who hurts you so deeply that he doesn't deserve a second thought, not a flicker of emotion…and to forgive him. Would Gabriel not do the same? Would she extend her hand to him if he was reaching out for hers now?"

"Rachel, I remember the War in Heaven as if it was yesterday — and Gabriel would never help him."

"Never?"

Raphael's face was one of stone. *"Never."*

MICHAEL

Rome

General Dante Carter moved through the massive throng of panicked people; a squadron of soldiers moved swiftly behind him. He was an athletic-looking man in his early forties. He had a strikingly handsome face, chiseled features, and intense, blue eyes — eyes that said, "I see the world differently. I have seen its beauties and I have seen its horrors. *I see you...*"

The look on his face was severe. He moved with determination through the wounded and the dead, trying to avoid the group of reporters chasing behind his every footstep.

"General! General!"

A microphone was thrust in his face, "General! It looks like World War III has hit the entire globe! What steps is the United Nations taking to help with the situation?"

He shoved the microphone away.

The situation...What's wrong with these people? Mass suicide, fiery hail, blood everywhere...this is more than a situation. He continued moving forward. He turned his head to one of the men beside him, "Get rid of them."

The soldier immediately broke away from the group. He and a few of the other soldiers blocked the reporters' paths, blocking them with their weapons. The throng of reporters stopped moving but their shouts continued on, "General Carter!"

How he hated reporters.

Carter entered a tent designated as Command Central. Inside, various computers, grids, maps and television monitors were set up displaying the city areas and news broadcasts from across the globe. Carter stepped in front of one of the city grids and pointed to three different locations commanding a soldier beside him, "Set up D-Mort here, here and here. Cold Zone here." The soldier relayed the message into a radio.

Carter moved to the back of the tent and sat down. He scoured reports strewn all over his designated table. His eyes narrowed in concentration as he read. Explosions. Riots. Mass suicide. Mobs. It was the same all over the world and there was no end in sight. It had been a long day and it was going to be an even longer night.

Carter set his reading aside and leaned back against his chair; his body was drenched in sweat; the humid temperature stifled the air inside the tent. He lifted his hand to wipe the sweat from his brow and stopped in mid-gesture. *What the...*

His breath fogged on the warm air. His body stilled in the realization. A cold wind gently blew across his papers. He quickly rose from his seat and grabbed hold of them, trying to keep them from flying away. He stood there — waiting. And then he heard it, the softest of whispers, *"For the kingdom, the claimant, the master..."* And then it was gone.

Carter did not move. He rapidly looked all around the tent. No one else seemed to notice the dramatic shift in temperature or even the strange whispers that heralded all around him. He focused on their mouths. His was the only one whose breath continued to fog on the humid air. His breathing slowed. Carter did not question his senses or give into the rationale that he was imaging things because of one solid fact: *this happened once before...* Carter was thinking rapidly, *where is the cold coming from?* And then the realization came.

Carter slowly turned his head and looked behind him. He moved the cloth away from the tent and saw a man standing directly on the other side. There was no one else around. The man's back was to him; he stood absolutely still. His long pale hair reached halfway down his back. Carter looked the man up and down, taking in the dark colors of his attire. He noticed that the man did not appear to be breathing. And yet, Carter continued to see his own breath fogging on the heat-filled air.

He looked back at the man. The man turned his head to the side, and what Carter saw chilled him to the bone. *His eye was solid black.* Carter continued to stand there, paralyzed. A slight curl formed on the pale-haired man's lips. The man turned his head forward and moved through the base camp gliding through it. As the man passed through, not a single soldier in the camp took notice of him.

Carter continued to watch the man move until he saw the pale-hair disappear into an alley at the other end of the camp.

"General."

Carter jumped. He dropped the cloth from the tent and turned back to the activity inside. "What is it?"

"The square is on fire."

Suddenly, hail rocketed inside the tent smashing everything in sight. Carter roared, *"EVERYONE OUT!"*

Carter and the rest of the soldiers rushed outside. The tent burst into flame. Carter stared at the inferno where he sat just moments before. Nothing of Command Central remained. He shifted his eyes to the darkened alley as the hail continued to pound against the world all around him.

This was far more than a mere situation…I've seen that man before.

*   *   *

Moloch and his band of demons continued dancing amidst the fire and blood, rioting over the birth of the first plague on their street. They knew that a domino effect of all the other plagues would soon follow. It had been prophesized. It had been feared. It had become reality. It was what they have been waiting for.

Yes…Lucifer was right.

Their fight to destroy humanity would one day bring heaven down to them to finish what was started so long ago. Yes, God loved his creation. He made them creators. He elevated them above the angels. And look at them now: hallowed-out souls made in the image of their Father groveling on the street — and not one of them called upon God's name.

How ironic. Their groans were the same here as they were in hell. And this street was still in the realm of the living. Just wait until these souls were carried through the gate of the inferno…*the bells shall ring for them.* Moloch's red beady eyes narrowed in lustful desire of what he would do to these humans once their souls came to his lair. *For he hates. He hates. He hates. He hates them.* It was then that he felt the cold wind blow through the street as his master whispered to him a name — a name that meant warning, *"Michael…Michael…"*

Moloch whipped his sword from his sheath and cawed loudly to his brood. The fallen angels fell silent; they quickly reached for their weapons. Their doll-like eyes searched the sky, the shadows, the rubble.

Michael.

It was bad enough when Gabriel was here, but Michael…Michael would annihilate them with a single swipe of his adamantine sword. But why this street? Moloch continued to search the landscape for the archangel. *"We feel him…we curse him…we know…"*

He did not call out to Michael, for to speak his name was a battle cry in the name of God. And no fallen angel would want him here. This could only mean one thing…someone here did. He turned toward the bodies lying on the street. It was then that he saw the body of a woman. She clutched her St. Michael's medal on her necklace. *It is she…it is she…it is she* who called to God for help. And God answered her. He sent her Michael.

Moloch's red, beady eyes rapidly searched the street high and low for the foe the dark, silky voice warned them against. The cold wind blew past him toward the shadows of the alley — and it was out of the shadow that the Prince of Angels came forth.

If Moloch had a heart, it would have stopped the moment he saw the outline of Michael's massive ten-foot frame in the darkness of the alley. Even from where he stood, Moloch could feel Michael's amber eyes on him. He could see Michael's muscular arms draped across his massive chest memorizing his targets before he engaged — and Moloch knew they were the targets.

Chills ran down Moloch's hunched spine as he watched all six of Michael's emerald wings emerge from his body. Their width was three times that of a condor — and they were no ordinary wings. They were eyes. They were arms. They were weapons. They were shields. No other angel could use their wings like him, for no other angel could fight like Michael. He was God's greatest warrior — his champion. And here he was, walking toward them.

With each step he took, the demons lost more of their courage; they lost the joy of their victorious dance. And just like the humans moments ago, they too had nowhere to go. There was no shelter that would hide them from this archangel.

With one final step, Michael's mighty foot landed on the street. It sent forth a vibration that could be felt in the demons' bellies — for the mighty archangel, rarely seen, was now upon the earth — and he didn't look happy.

Michael took in the sight of the street. His yellow-green eyes were like a laser beam scanning everything before him, memorizing it, until those eyes landed on the demons.

Michael looked down upon them with the eyes of a hunter who had found his prey. Moloch and the other demons backed away from the alley, falling into each other, scaling back on their hands and knees as they moved. Never taking his eyes off the demons on the street, Michael's wings quickly retracted into his body, revealing a squadron of angelic warriors behind him. The fallen ones cackled and cawed in fear and anger at the sight of the soldiers before them.

Without a single word, Michael nodded to his right. A flood of Virtues flew to the right. He nodded to the left; more Virtues followed suit. His carefully sculpted face looked forward, and the remaining angels behind him — Thrones — rolled their bodies over into circular wheels. Their bodies ignited in fire as they rushed past Michael and onto the street, steamrolling the hail and extinguishing the fire. Their bodies unraveled at the feet of a group of hookers. They stood upright and transformed into police officers appearing to the lost men and women out of nowhere. They rushed the group of humans out of the storm to a place of shelter.

The virtues, the miracle workers, were angels notorious for shifting their shape. They dropped from the sky and ran onto the street shifting into the form of firemen, paramedics, and doctors administering to the souls still there. Moloch watched as they worked their miracles of treating the injured, lifting the dying, and protecting the forsaken. He raged at the sight, *"Ours! Ours! Ours!"*

Moloch heard the sound of hail crunching behind him. He whirled around only to see Michael standing directly behind him. His red goat-like eyes narrowed in fury.

"They are ours. They are married to nothingness, Prince of Angels. They are for the kingdom…"

Michael simply nodded his head in reply, motioning for Moloch to look to the sky. Moloch followed his gaze just in time to see warrior angels dive down upon him and his band of demons from above. The warriors slammed down on top of them pummeling them into the ground, sending Moloch and the rest back to their lair in hell.

Michael breathed deeply. He looked all around, taking in the destruction on the streets surrounding him, watching as the hail continued to rocket down from the sky.

"Don't kill me!"

Michael turned and saw a drug addict crouched beside a dumpster; the young man was wasted away to mere bones. He trembled violently as he looked into the eyes of the archangel, for he had seen the unseen. The building above the young man burst into flames as the fiery hail continued to pulverize anything and everything in its path. The young man fell forward from the force of the impact.

Crawling on his hands and knees, he headed straight for Michael. He grabbed onto Michael's enormous foot and prostrated himself down before the archangel. With dilated, terrified eyes, the man looked up at him and pleaded, "Please, don't kill me."

Michael moved his foot from the young man's grasp. He looked down at the addict with enraged eyes. "Do not do it! Do not kneel before me, mortal man, for I am a fellow servant of yours and one of your brothers of the earth. Kneel before God and worship him alone. *Now, get up!*"

The addict lifted his head and slowly stood. Michael locked eyes with the young man. The silent communication that passed between them slowed the man's shakes until his body was calmed by slow, even breaths. The man stepped away from Michael and ran through the fire and the hail out of the street and into the night, forever changed by his encounter with the archangel.

Michael watched him go. It was through the young man's path that Michael saw the work of the angels under his command and was pleased. Tears had stopped; panic had died; and those in need of help had received it. Michael continued to walk down the street taking it all in.

He stopped dead in his tracks.

His eyes narrowed as he tried to decipher what he saw before him. Amongst the hail and blood in the street, was a scarlet feather — *Gabriel's feather.*

He strode toward it with powerful steps unwilling to believe the feather lying there was real. Michael bent down and picked it up. As he caressed the feather between his fingers, he searched for the answers to his questions as to how her feather came to be there and why.

From the far recesses of his mind a memory came forth. A memory so long forgotten that Michael's breath quickened at the suddenness to which it had revealed itself — as if this memory alone wanted to be remembered, shouting that it should never have been forgotten. And it was of Gabriel. Beautiful Gabriel with her raven hair and sable eyes. The fierceness of her beauty and the regality of her demeanor was one that always commanded respect and alluded to the knowledge that you were the lucky one if you were invited into the confidence she shared with none. In the midst of that memory, he saw her...

"Michael, he is my friend, my greatest friend, before the hierarchy, before the army, before oaths and duty. I will protect him by all means I know how..."

As soon as he remembered it, a feeling of dread consumed him. There were demons on this street when he arrived. Had Gabriel been here, that would not be. The people here were defenseless when he stepped out of the alley and onto the street. Had Gabriel been here, that could not be for she would have summoned a squadron of angels here to protect the humans as she had always done since the birth of mankind. *But she knows...* and the evidence that she knew was like a slap in the face that she had been here and done... *nothing.*

Looking at the fire raining down around him, gripping her feather in his hand, Michael fought the thoughts, *would she help him? Would she do this?* But the answer did not come. Tightening his fist around her feather, he forced the doubt from his mind. *No, she would not do it. Not for him. Not after that moment.* Not after what Lucifer had done, for Michael remembered it. But then, in the remembering he thought on the things that once were before they turned into the things they had become. Therein lay the doubt and the thoughts came again. *Has she helped him when she should not? Has she broken the chain of command and sought escape in the shadow, away from God's light?*

For all the centuries that Gabriel had been his second in command, Michael was suddenly saddened by the fact that he knew her not. She confided in him not. Her mind was her own, only open for the Father to see, for the father to fill, for the father to know. But it was not always so. There was one other whom she invited in. Thinking on them the way they were — Gabriel and Lucifer — remembering it, Michael could not shake the feeling of doom that had crept up on him this day on this street.

"To entertain the idea, Gabriel, of going against God's plans is an abomination and disgrace to the word 'angel'."

Michael remembered her face at that moment — a dual mask of sadness and hope. How much she wanted to believe that Lucifer would return to the kingdom of his Father's throne; how much Michael wanted to believe it for her, for her heart at that moment — with all its resilience — was breaking. Had it not been for the hope he had seen in her eyes that day, he would have thwarted Lucifer's ultimate plan long before it came to fruition. And yet, after all this time…would she try to help him once again?

The Prince of Angels emerged in the world today to fight against this mystery, for the plague was not meant to come this day — the Father had told him so. The time had not yet come. Michael emerged onto the street believing the answer to the mystery originated in hell, but seeing this crimson feather of one so close, his heart was deeply troubled. The last time a trail of feathers had been found was in heaven when Lucifer had abandoned hope of God's will for his purpose. And with each feather that had fallen from Lucifer's opaque wings, there remained a trail of sorrow.

Michael looked at the bloodied ground scorched in fire. Feeling the coarseness of Gabriel's feather between his fingertips, he closed his amber eyes and breathed in long and deep. There was only one way to know the answer.

With the feather still clutched in his hand, Michael slowly rose to standing. It was then that he feels their heated eyes upon him.

Michael turned toward the end of the street where he sensed their presence. And there, in the shadows of the street was another brood of fallen angels; and at the head was their leader, the Herculean cherub — *Gokor.*

Gokor's battle-axe rested at his side, his one remaining wing black as coal. There were five fallen angels altogether standing behind him and they were all armed.

Gokor and Michael stared at one another — champions of their

day when they stood together in the light — rivals of old. Gokor's burnt lips pulled back in a snarl. He growled, "Our day has come, Prince of Angels."

"Not this day, fallen one."

Gokor's smile faded into a sharp grimace. He swung his battle-axe over his head, crouching into a bull's stance ready to charge. The fallen angels behind him followed suit. "We shall see, *prince*."

Gokor took a step forward, ready to advance upon Michael, when twelve warrior angels dropped from the sky directly behind Michael. Their swords were drawn, their bows strung, their aim ready.

Gokor froze, doing the math as he took in the situation that had now presented itself. He lowered his axe. "I shall see you again. *Soon...*"

Demons replied, *"Soon...in the kingdom."*

Gokor raised his elk horn; he blew into it calling to the remainder of the demons on the street hiding in the shadows. Hearing the summons, they scattered onto the street from all sides and rushed past Michael and the warrior angels as quickly as they could — jumping, slithering, and creeping along the way.

"To the kingdom...we go in hate."

"We go...prince of angels...we go."

"We go to Cain's father."

"To the Lord of Death we go...to him!"

"Him!"

"Him!"

Climbing into the shadows behind Gokor, he and his brood crept back into the darkness from whence they came. Still looking into the darkness, Michael commanded the squadron, "Angels! Return to the heavens!"

In unison, the warrior angels pounded their fists into their breastplates in salute and launched into the sky. Michael opened his hand and looked down at Gabriel's feather. His jaw clenched as he closed his fist tightly around it. His six emerald wings extended; he rocketed into the sky.

A SECRET

Eastern Desert

G abriel dropped out of the nighttime sky slamming down onto the sands of the eastern desert below. She raced toward the spot where she buried her trumpet so long ago. Hail covered the ground turning areas of the sand red from the blood-saturated rain. Small fires burned upon the sand reminding Gabriel of the tune that had just been played.

Gabriel calmed her breathing, focusing her mind on the ground below. She extended her hands out over the sand attempting to summon the ark, aiming all of her energy toward it, hoping against hope that what she already knew could not possibly be true.

Sand upon sand pushed upward from the spot where the ark was buried. Gabriel concentrated harder, feverishly trying to call to it, but all that continued to surface was the miniscule particles of endless sand. She dropped to her knees mentally exhausted. The melodious voice returned, *"Gabriel...beloved..."*

She closed her eyes to the seductive voice when a different one called her name. *"GABRIEL!"*

Her eyes snapped open.

"What have you done?"

Gabriel clenched her jaw at the sound of Michael's voice. She slowly stood, keeping her back to him. "You already know, Michael."

She ruffled her wings to rid herself of the dust on her feathers as they retracted into her body. Gabriel turned to face her commander. The moment he saw her pale face, Michael's spirit plummeted to the ground. He took in her altered, withered appearance, and her eyes…*haunted. Restless.* He had seen eyes like that before. *It cannot be…*

Several moments passed before he spoke. "You are my second in command, Gabriel."

She pounded her fist into her chest and stood at attention. "I am, Michael. What is our Father's will?"

Michael studied her face. "Where is your bow?" Gabriel remained silent. "Did you bury that for Satan to find as well?"

The slightest flicker of rage burst forth from behind her eyes. A slight curl formed at the ends of her lips. With the calmest tone, she simply answered, "No."

Michael crossed his massive arms across his broad chest. "Our Father has given orders for you and the other five to remain on the earth to protect the people from the coming plagues — at all costs. And make no mistake…all of the plagues will come."

He lifted his arm and opened his hand. She looked down and saw her feather. Her face softened. Michael watched her reaction, but Gabriel gave nothing away. She took it from him.

"And what about my trumpet?"

Michael dropped his arms to his sides as he stepped toward Gabriel so that their faces were inches apart. "If you wanted it so badly, you should have held onto it instead of handing it over to the devil! It is no longer *yours*, Gabriel!"

She lifted her head; her tired eyes suddenly ignited in flame. She roared back, *"IT'S FOREVER MINE!"* Her voice resonated in the night.

They continued to stare each other down until Michael finally spoke. "The people of the earth are your priority now." He looked at her as if he was looking upon a different kind of angel. "Gabriel, do you know what you've done?!?"

She looked away from his accusing stare. "I've done nothing that shouldn't have been done long ago."

Michael was so stunned by her answer that he could barely speak. "You are not the judge over the people of the earth." When Gabriel did not respond, his anger rose. "You do realize that you have set things in motion that cannot be undone! Whatever possessed you to bury your trumpet, your most treasured gift from the Father, whatever the intent, has been used as a key to open the door to destruction before it was ready to walk through the door! Gabriel, the followers of God could lose their lives over this. They have not been given His seal to protect them. There was not yet a need to give it! The plagues can affect them as they would an enemy of God." Michael's eyes bored into hers, "How could you not think this could happen? *You* above all others. He watches you, Gabriel, or had you forgotten?"

She looked up at him with a look of such betrayal that Michael was almost ashamed that he asked the question. He had no reason to doubt her actions. He trusted no other angel like he trusted her. That was why it angered him so tremendously that Gabriel refused to speak a single word in reply.

"Gabriel…"

She lowered her head. "Of course I haven't forgotten. Michael…" Gabriel looked up at him as if she was about to tell him everything. But just as she was about to speak, the cold wind came.

Her gaze shifted to the breeze and her eyes closed. As soon as the wind passed, she looked almost sad. But then again, before Lucifer fell, so did he.

Finally, void of any emotion, she replied, "What of the antichrist?"

"The Soulless One is biding his time and using it to his full advantage; the way he was meant to. That is how he will succeed for a time…he will come upon the people like a thief in the night." Michael's anger rose as he spoke the words of the prophecy. He turned back to Gabriel, studying her. For once she could not hold his stare. She lowered her head.

Michael hated this. It had been billions of years since they had last fought, yet the reason now was the same. *"I have to go to him. I have to try. If I'm not back by the time you sound the horn, come for me, Michael..."* He had sounded that horn and she had not come.

He tried to block out the memory. "I came here to collect you."

"Where are we going?"

"Rome."

Gabriel nodded to her commander, pounding her fist into her chest in salute. Their six seraphim wings expanded and the archangels took flight — all evidence of their visit was gone, save for Gabriel's feather; it rested upon the sand amidst the hail and blood.

From underneath her feather, a scaly, snake-like hand with long black claws emerged and pulled it back down into the sand below.

"Beloved..."

An evil laugh bellowed from hell.

PAID IN FULL

Rome

Jonathan stood by the fireplace in his hotel suite in Rome looking at a photograph carefully placed on the mantle. The photo was of Rachel's mother Julia. It was taken at a moment in life when he remembered her best: beautiful, healthy, and happy — a glimpse of what her life held before it ended.

Jonathan picked up the frame and looked at it as if the photograph were merely a window instead of an ink-filled image of his dead wife behind a wooden frame. He stared at it, knowing he had no one to blame for the present predicament he was in but himself, for he walked the path directly to it. And there was no turning back. There was no escape for him.

"Help her." He took the frame in his hands, "Help our daughter, Julia. Help her see it through to the end."

He knew though, it was not only up to Rachel — *he* could still change it. He knew *he* could still try to find a way to help his daughter himself. *Free will*...but Jonathan knew he never would. *Would she even do it?* He had no answer. And with the sudden realization that he knew so little about his own daughter, his body grew weary in despair. Leaving Rachel all alone with the task of fixing his mistake

80

she knew nothing about, never knowing his motive, he knew he was nothing but a coward.

Cradling the photograph in his arms, Jonathan slowly lifted his head to look out the hotel window. His face changed from one of pained memory to fear and anguish as he watched the hail and fire continue to cascade down from the sky like gently falling snow.

He closed his eyes in anguish. *The plagues...the plagues are here. Hail and fire mixed with blood — and you have brought it. But I will bring no more. I will not herald a melody that will cause a third of the sea to become a crimson tide. I will not be blamed for a third of the living creatures in the sea to die or for the waters of the earth to be made bitter. I cannot bear to watch the sky become dark or observe a swarm of locusts hunt human beings in order to sting and kill. And the riders...more death...until the great earthquake comes.*

Jonathan turned toward the window. Through the falling flames, he could see a figure barreling forth. Jonathan squinted his eyes, trying to make out the form. It was then he recognized the blackened wings, the flaming eyes. Felix was flying toward him; the scroll was clutched tightly in his deformed hand. Jonathan's breath began to fog.

"You *are* to blame." He shifted his gaze to Beelzebub standing in the shadows of the room. "You said...*yes.*"

And as fast as the self-absolution came, it was gone. Make God pay. Make God answer. An eye for an eye. Jonathan lowered his head in despair.

Fire and hail slammed through the window spraying shards of glass all across the room as Felix burst through. The suite caught fire but Jonathan did not move. Instead, he looked at the photo of his beloved wife resting in his hands.

Smoke flooded the interior of the room; Jonathan didn't even try to escape. He remained before the hearth, inhaling the deadly fumes until his body ultimately collapsed. The photograph of his wife burned in the fire inches from his face.

Beelzebub watched without a flicker of emotion. *"I...see...you..."*

Blue flames ignited from within the hearth. Beelzebub turned his blackened eyes to it. The melodious voice spoke a command, *"Bring his soul to hell...ring the bells."*

KILLING TIME

Oxford University

"No sign of my father."

Rachel read the text from her phone.

"Who's it from?"

"Gail, my father's secretary." She continued reading.

"Have you tried calling Ben?"

Rachel looked at him. "No, I'd rather not open the chapter in that book again."

"But he would know. He's always with your father on his expeditions."

She ignored him and went back to reading the text. "Gail said my father left the site two weeks ago. I highly doubt Ben went with him." Rachel clicked off her screen. "My father could be dead for all I know. I just wish I could reach him, change his mind, and stop him from what he is going to do — *if* he hasn't done it already."

Rachel picked up her notes on Raphael's translation of the parchment. "*'To call upon my name to lead them to it?'* What would ever possess my father to call upon the devil? Why do this? Something so unimaginable — like it was a bad dream. I knew, Raphael, that he hated God…that he hated me. I know he has. That's why he stays away from me, never speaks to me."

"Rachel…"

She smiled sadly at Raphael. "I know what you're going to say: that he doesn't hate me; that he's in pain; that deep down he loves me, but he just can't get in front of his grief to show me. I know all the psychological babble and I will not allow him an excuse or way out of all the pain and hurt that he has caused *me*. And you know, it's me who should hate him for all he has done. And I never have."

Raphael remained silent.

"He can't undo it — not any of it. He can't bring my mother back. And how I wish he could." Rachel started to cry but fought back the tears as her chin began to tremble. "Because I don't know how to be. I lost my example of what a woman is supposed to be like. I never believed in angels, Raphael, but if I did, my mother would have been one." She wiped the tears from her face. "And here I thought the hardest thing in my life was battling the scars of being left behind by the loss of my mother and the neglect of my father. And now this. This has been one hell of a birthday, let me tell you." She looked at the scroll lying on the desk. "What I can't figure out is why my father sent this to me. *Keep it safe*. Safe from what?"

"Plagues, Rachel. Safe from the plagues."

Rachel contemplated what he was saying. "His note was almost like a prayer." She was lost in thought. "Did I ever tell you that after my mother's funeral, I stood over her coffin before they lowered her into the ground? And *I* prayed...I prayed, Raphael, that God would grant me *one* miracle. That he would raise my mother from the dead the way his son raised his friend Lazarus — simply because I asked. It was more for my father than for me..." She laughed softly. "The hope of miracles is a cruel reality when you know that they don't apply to you. They lowered her coffin to the ground and I haven't prayed since."

Through the hole in the ceiling, hail suddenly rained down. Raphael saw the tiny pebbles accumulating on the floor. Seeing them covered in blood, he knew what it meant.

"Raphael, there's hail in our office."

"And blood." He turned and looked at her. "Satan has the trumpet. Your father is with the fallen ones. He has played the first tune."

"But how? *I* had the sheet with the notes!"

"Perhaps he memorized the first tune. He did have the sheet first, you know." Seeing the hole in the ceiling, the bookshelves turned over and the furniture on fire, he clenched his fists in frustration. He quickly looked back at the monitor, memorizing its words.

"Raphael, what happens if my father plays all the tunes?"

"Armageddon, Rachel — that's what it means."

The fire alarm went off triggering the sprinkler system. Raphael watched the water pour down onto the shambles of his once-immaculate office. He cringed. Rachel caught his look. "Heaven must be impeccably clean."

"Immaculate." Raphael continued to read the script on the monitor.

"So how do we get the sheet back before my father plays the final tune?"

"It's not the music sheet we need — it's the trumpet."

A heavenly light suddenly appeared and beamed down upon Raphael from the hole in the ceiling. He looked up to it. Rachel looked up to it too, unsure where the light was coming from or what it meant. It glittered all around her pouring over her like a shower of diamonds. She extended her hands to it. *So beautiful...*

As suddenly as the light appeared, it was gone. Raphael's face had changed from one of distress to one of confidence. He looked at Rachel. "Let's go."

"Where? *Hell?*" There was a look of horror on her face.

"No, Rome...to see some friends of mine."

Raphael's six sapphire wings jutted out from his back. He scooped Rachel up into his arms.

"We're flying?"

"Yes, we're flying."

He launched them into the sky.

THE LAWLESS ONE

Rome

Draped in the shadows of the night, Carter stood in a darkened alley hidden from view. He looked out at the emergency camp watching the swarm of faces of the hopeless, the lost, and the fearful. He watched them all: U.N. soldiers, first responders, everyday civilians and tourists as they milled about the Cold Zone. He studied their actions and reactions, watching as some moved faster than others, attempting to keep every aspect of their world from turning completely upside down from the catastrophe that had been brought this day.

Carter had been in Rome for over a year now; he was the first one the U.N. called when the plague hit. Even *he* recognized that it was a plague. What a shame no one else did — they merely thought it was a "situation." Every person he had encountered in the emergency camp had been seemingly rendered helpless and dumb in a city surrounded by religious edifice and artifact. Their desperate energy was so overwhelming, threatening to suck him down into a black hole that he needed this moment to get away from them all, to breathe the air around him fresh and clear rather than the stifling stench of the crowd. But that's not the only reason he was in the alley.

Where is the pale-haired man?

After Command Central went up in flames, they set up another one. Carter had reviewed the tapes of the surrounding area looking for the man. But what he saw on film, just before the tent caught fire, made no sense. Carter watched himself pull the cloth away from the tent…but there was no one standing on the other side.

Not possible.

But Carter knew what he had seen. And he knew it was true. He had been waiting for such a sign for a long, long time. And now it had come.

Carter continued watching from the alley, watching as everyone beyond it clung to their humanity, finally aware of their mortality, and terrified in the realization that their time was running out — but not for him. For him, time was just beginning. The emergence of the pale-haired man told him it was so.

Carter had seen the man only once before. He was fifteen years old, living in his adopted parents' home in Austria. He was up late practicing his violin. His parents always made him practice: musical instruments, languages, martial arts. But he didn't mind. Learning was easy for him. Sleep was unnecessary. And knowledge was power.

On that particular winter's night, a cold breeze had blown through his room. He still remembered the feeling — *almost like a gentle caress.* It cradled him like a mother to a son, and then moved swiftly on. *Where had it come from? And where did it go?* Having been touched so suddenly by that long-forgotten breeze, he longed to have it hold him once more.

Carter remembered looking all around the room, looking for the open window that brought the draft, but there wasn't a single window open. He walked outside his room, down the hall, checking all the rest of the windows and doors in the house. They were all closed. That was when he saw it: a blue glow coming from inside the library. He opened the door and saw the indigo flames burning inside the fireplace. And standing in front of the sapphire blaze was the same pale-haired man. His eyes were black as coal. The man did not speak. He simply looked Dante up and down. Having eyes such as those examine him was an unnerving experience. It almost made him mad.

"Who are you?"

"Who I am does not matter. It is who you are and what you will become that matters most." A small smile had formed on the man's face; but then he lowered his eyes to Dante's heart and the smile disappeared. *"You...feel...nothing..."*

"I never have."

Carter never forgot that moment. The man had looked at him with his lifeless eyes. Eyes that reflected the emotions of his very own soul — if he had one, that is. "What a pity," the man said. "You will never know what you have to lose. You will never know God."

Dante's eyes had narrowed in confusion. He scoffed at the man, "Know God? The only gods that exist are self-made men. And I intend to become one of them."

Dante smiled smugly at the man, priding himself on his confidence and intelligence, but he did not get the reaction he expected. Most of the time, he either got scolded for his arrogance, was commended by the scientific elite his parents held court with, or was ridiculed against by his younger religious peers. The pale-haired man, however, gave no reaction at all. He simply stared at him with those creepy eyes. Then he said the strangest thing, "Enemy."

Dante did not know how to respond. It was then that the pale-haired man pulled a scroll from inside his long, dark cloak and handed it to Dante.

"What is this?"

"Your legacy. It was written by my master. All the prophecies of your existence listed on a single piece of paper. Memorize it. Recognize the signs, for I will come again."

Looking down at the parchment in his hands, Dante's heart began to beat rapidly. It was the first time he felt it — excitement — and then something deeply rooted within his heart burned and slowly began to grow. *Desire. Ambition.* At that moment, he remembered looking up at the pale-haired man yearning to learn more. The man was studying him.

"Who am I?"

"You are nothing more than a key to a door I long to pass through."

That was when the cold wind returned and cradled him once more. The flames in the hearth blazed brightly. Dante had turned his gaze to it and heard the wind speak, *"Mine...mine...mine...for the kingdom..."*

Dante immediately felt the reply pour forth from his lips, "For the kingdom..."

The pale-haired man narrowed his onyx-colored eyes at him, "What a pity indeed."

And then they were gone — the wind, the fire, the man. How long he had been waiting to see him again, to feel the cold breeze on his face.

Carter took a long drag off his cigarette.

He had studied that scroll. But that wasn't all he studied; he studied history, politics, war, the rise and fall of great men. No matter how much he read, he craved knowing more. How Carter longed to have a history, a lifeline to belong to, but he was merely an orphan never knowing who he truly was or where he had come from. The scroll, however, gave him a history to embrace, a point of origin to start from and the reminder to keep going. And going he did. He studied the kings, the dictators, and all the famous generals of the world. How he loved Alexander — a man after his own heart — a man of charisma, a man of power, a man who ruled his world. He had studied them all — their successes, their failures, but what he loved to study most of all were the emperors: Nero, Constantine...*too bad Caesar never became one.*

And the scroll...the scroll had said he would enter into politics. But politics was nothing more to him than a chess game getting you where you wanted to be by outsmarting the other opponent. And to be like the men he admired, the great men of history, the political arena was inevitable. But he didn't want to be like most politicians of present day — men who had never seen a war, never served in the military, and only ruled because they were ruled by other men; he didn't want to be a tyrant either — he wanted to be loved. Love got people to do things willingly. Ruling by fear got people to do things as well, but that route would require more work to keep the people from ultimately turning on him in the end. And he had too much to do than worry about that — *according to that scroll.*

As he grew older he recognized that people wanted to feel important, respected, appreciated. As a man, women were attracted to him and men wanted to be like him, so using people to get what he wanted was easy — so long as they were a part of whatever he was doing; so long as they felt important, respected, appreciated — they never knew they were being used. But when he entered the military, the desire to be his own man and rule others rose once again. The only way to do it on a massive scale was to be what all the great men before him had become. So that's exactly what he did. He became a general.

Looking out from the alley at all the news crews, he knew this moment was his opportunity. *I'll have to learn to like them only to use them.* He could see the steps before him and knew the climb would be swift.

After all this time…

Carter breathed in long and deep. Looking out at the city, he realized that this was the moment he had been waiting for to embrace what he truly desired: peace. *Years* of peace. It was only through seven years of it that he could finish the race of his life and achieve his final goal — the one he was born for. The mere fact that he could hide amongst the shadows at a moment like this, he knew that it was simple metaphor for what he ultimately aimed to do. And it would be the magnum opus of all created symphonies that the world had ever encountered.

Carter finished his cigarette and tossed it to the ground. Standing in the shadows with not a camera on him, not a soldier needing command, not a civilian or tourist in need of comfort, he leaned against the adjacent wall and thought, *What was the man doing in the alley?*

Not quite ready to give up his place of solitude, he remained in the dark knowing that this very spot would remain uninhabited; there was too much happening for anyone to want to be alone at a time like this. And then he saw him...

The pale-haired man moved slowly through the crowd, gliding directly toward the alley. His blackened eyes never shifted direction as he moved with an eerie grace — eyes...black as the darkest night. *Dead eyes. Doll's eyes. I remember those eyes.*

As confident as Carter was, the look of the pale-haired man caused him to shift uneasily; he backed further into the shadows without realizing it. His foot knocked against something hard on the ground behind him. He looked down but could make nothing out.

He lowered down to the ground and knelt beside an object at his feet. Carter took his lighter out and flicked it on. At that moment, his radio sounded. "General, we're moving the carcass to D-Mort."

Carter unclipped the radio from his belt and raised it to his lips. "Roger that."

The last thing that was heard was the faint sound of a metal box opening.

ROME

Raphael landed just outside of the Sistine Chapel. Rachel was clasping onto his shirt, clutching it for dear life. Her eyes were glued shut.

"Rachel, you can let go now."

"Are we on the ground?"

"Yes, we are on the ground." He uncurled her fingers from around his collar and lowered her down. "I had no idea you were afraid of flying."

Rachel turned her head away from the destruction. "Not when I'm in a *plane*, Raphael — in a *plane*." It took her a few moments to center herself.

The sun had set over the city. All around her the scene was the same as the one before: fire and hail rained down from the sky above. *Chaos*. People were running to and fro; running for shelter, running from death. The square was on fire; the blood from the hail had painted the streets a dark syrupy red. She turned around and saw the chapel. "We're meeting your friends *here*?"

"Yes." He started to walk through the chapel entrance.

"Wait...I thought I was your only friend."

Raphael turned around. His gray eyes danced with amusement. "You would think that."

Rachel scowled at him. "My point is: who are these people and can we trust them?"

Raphael smiled confidently. "Step inside, Miss Devereaux, and find out for yourself." But before they entered the chapel, Rachel's cell phone rang. She answered it. "Gail!" The look on her face as she listened to the caller's voice was one that Raphael knew would soon be coming. Rachel's face paled; her eyes had a far-off look to them. "Thank you." She clicked off the phone and turned to Raphael. "My father is dead. They found his body in a hotel room — here in Rome."

"I'm sorry, Rachel."

She looked at him, her eyes finally blinking in comprehension as the news settled in. "Don't be." Rachel looked around at her surroundings, not sure if she should stay or go. But where does one go to bury a father that buried himself years ago? There was nothing left to do but the one thing that was left undone: his last request — *keep it safe*.

Raphael rested his hands on her shoulders. "You are always free to choose your own way, even when outside elements try to force your path."

She touched his hand. Taking a deep breath, Rachel made a decision. "Let's go inside, Raphael."

"You don't have to."

She turned around and faced him, a calmness had set behind her eyes — the first in a long while. "My father wanted me to keep the scroll safe so that no more plagues would come. I'm going to finish what he started — with or without it. I'm going to make it right. And I need you to protect me to do it. At least, that's what God told you to do, right? I mean, you are an *arch*angel."

Raphael smiled faintly, "Right."

Rachel took one last breath, buried her emotions deep inside — a survival skill she learned long ago — and followed Raphael through the chapel doors.

*   *   *

The moment they entered the chapel, Michelangelo's brilliant frescos came into view. Standing with his back to them, Rachel could make out the outline of a giant, athletic-looking man. The man did not turn upon their arrival, but stared straight ahead concentrating on something else up ahead giving it his undivided attention.

As they walked closer toward the man, Rachel could see his broad, muscular shoulders and brown wavy hair that rested just above them. Every line of his body was chiseled to perfection exuding power, strength, and grace. The mere sight of his ten-foot frame was overwhelming — surreal.

Raphael approached the man's side and pounded his fist into his chest in salute. "Michael."

Michael.

Rachel could barely believe it as she looked upon the powerful archangel. Michael turned toward Raphael and grinned — even his teeth were perfectly molded. Various images passed through her mind: a statue of Michael aiming his sword down upon the devil under his feet; the painting of Domenico Beccafumi's *The Archangel Michael Drives the Rebel Angels from Heaven*; God's greatest warrior — the one Homer must have been thinking of when he wrote about the Achilles…and *he's standing right in front of me.* Rachel's breath caught in her throat at the sight of his gorgeous face and amber eyes. *This man is beautiful.*

Almost as if he had heard her thoughts, Michael turned his head toward Rachel. The moment his eyes met hers, she froze, for his eyes were so penetrating that it was almost as if he was looking directly into her very soul, for his eyes were the kind that would never allow you to lie, for those eyes would know. Rachel could barely breathe as he looked at her.

"Michael, this is Rachel."

Michael bowed to her, "Rachel Julia Devereaux, beloved daughter of God, I am Michael."

Rachel's knees almost buckled out from underneath her as the

Prince of Angels bowed to her. She looked to Raphael hoping he would direct her on how to respond, but he merely smiled, amused by her sudden lack of words and nervousness. Not knowing what to do, Rachel curtsied in reply.

"She's usually not this quiet, Michael. I think she's overwhelmed by your beauty."

"Raphael!" She hit him.

Raphael merely grinned. "What news? Where are the others?"

"Uriel, Raguel, Sariel, and Jeremiel are guarding the souls in the West, North and South."

"And what of Gabriel?"

Gabriel.

Michael's jaw tightened. His face looked taught as he stepped aside. Several feet down the aisle of the chapel the archangel stood. Her back was to them as she stared up at *The Separation of Light from Darkness.*

The smile on Raphael's face faded.

If it weren't for her breathing, Raphael would have thought she was a shrunken statue carved to look like a mock rendition of the powerful archangel he had always known. Taking in Gabriel's ragged and withered appearance, worry and fear cast their shadows over his face. He glanced quickly at Michael willing an answer to be given by his commander. Michael held Raphael's stare but revealed nothing.

Rachel, never having seen Raphael look so distraught, touched his arm in concern. She whispered to him, "Raphael, what is it? You look like you've seen a ghost."

Raphael continued, "No, not a ghost…she looks like…"

"I know." Michael interrupted before Raphael could finish the thought.

"Hello, Raphael." Gabriel's husky voice filled the chapel. She had yet to move from her statuesque pose.

"Gabriel…"

Raphael released Rachel's hand and rushed toward Gabriel with hurried steps. He looked down at her pale face. What he saw when he looked into her eyes alarmed him. Her eyes had dark pools beneath them. Normally lit afire with a fierce light, her brown eyes had dulled. Seeing the look of distress on his face, Gabriel touched his cheek with her pale hand.

"Ah, Raphael. Do not be afraid of the image you see before you. I am merely tired." She looked up at the ceiling, breathing in long and deep. "The sight of these paintings calms me. History painted with brushes and oils onto mere walls beckoning to be remembered — days of old, moments long past — extraordinary people."

Rachel could hear Gabriel's voice — its texture: the sound of the purest tone — the kind of voice that made you *want* to listen just to hear it regardless of the message being spoken. She could think of only one word to describe Gabriel's voice: *intoxicating*.

Michael leaned against a pillar, his muscular arms folded across his massive chest. Willing herself to tear her eyes from the look of his biceps, she whispered to Michael, "Are female angels always so short?"

Without turning, he answered, "No. She is taller than Raphael. Gabriel is not well and the source of her ailment she will not say."

From the tense look on his face, Rachel could see the frustration and concern behind what Gabriel's silence truly communicated. She turned her attention back toward Raphael and Gabriel. Rachel still could not believe it. *Raphael...Michael...and now Gabriel.* Rachel pieced together the fragments of knowledge in her mind: bearer of good tidings, friend of Lucifer, second in command to Michael, respected by Raphael, feared by men, the angel who buried her trumpet that had now unleashed the first plague, the one who was to blame, the one who stood a few feet from her now — a shadow in the mist. She spoke her last thought aloud, *"The messenger."*

Michael turned his head to look at her, "Yes, she is. But the reasons for all that has come about she will not tell, for God has chosen his messenger well."

Rachel looked into his eyes and saw a look of pride in them as he spoke but also one of anger. Remembering Raphael's confidence behind Gabriel's ultimate intent on burying her trumpet and then seeing the intense look on Michael's face as he studied his second-in-command, she wondered... *Which side is Gabriel really on?* She looked back at Gabriel. *Oh crap.* Gabriel was looking directly at her. Rachel's breath stilled. *Did she hear me?* Their eyes locked.

Like a magnet, Rachel could not tear her eyes away from Gabriel's, for Gabriel's eyes were a wonder — a kaleidoscope of memory filled with the history of love and loss, an ocean of secrets masked by shields of glass swirling around each other like a black hole sucking you in. *Friend of Lucifer...*

"Rachel Julia Devereaux, beloved daughter of God..."

Upon hearing her name, Rachel felt as though she had never heard it before. The manner in which Gabriel pronounced it gave her name a heightened meaning — a feeling of greater importance. Without taking her eyes from Rachel's, Gabriel pointed to Cosimo Rosselli's, *Crossing the Red Sea.* "Did you know that Moses was a stutterer? And yet, it was he whom God called to command the sea and set a nation free."

Rachel's breath quickened as the sound of Gabriel's voice penetrated and absorbed into her every fiber, sinking into every layer of skin. She tried to look at the painting, but she could not pull her gaze away. Without turning her head, Gabriel pointed toward the painting of David and Goliath. "And then God chose a spirited five-foot-four young man to slay a giant descended from the Nephilim in order to become a king of kings."

As she talked she moved slowly toward Rachel until she was standing right in front of her. Gabriel stared at her, challenging Rachel to speak or utter a single word of the thoughts that were running through her head. But Rachel had suddenly become a mute, for Rachel had heard Gabriel's voice like no other — and it was hypnotizing.

Gabriel turned and raised her finger toward the direction of *The Last Judgment.* She leaned toward Rachel's ear and whispered, "And it was a fourteen-year-old girl with a faith that rivaled the angels who bore the son of my Father."

Rachel was finally able to shift her gaze away from Gabriel, but she quickly looked back at the archangel; Gabriel was studying her. What the archangel saw she did not say, for Gabriel revealed nothing. Without another word, Gabriel stood upright and walked back down the chapel in solitude, breathing in each and every painting on its walls and ceiling.

Michael remained silent, devouring Gabriel's every movement, every word, memorizing it for any clue into the heart of his second in command.

Gabriel ignored it all as she continued on, "And do you know what made them all extraordinary?" She looked back at Rachel waiting for an answer. Seeing that Rachel had none, Gabriel smiled fondly, "They didn't think that they were."

Gabriel looked at the paintings once more, speaking more to herself than to those around her, "Ordinary people made extraordinary because they moved with my Father so that the father's will could be done. There is no movement anymore."

Gabriel's eyes stung with tears; Raphael caught it. His face changed to one of sadness at seeing her inner sorrow at the memories painted above. *"Extraordinary people...*and so are you, Rachel Julia Devereaux, beloved daughter of God."

Gabriel turned and faced Rachel once again. Gabriel's eyes were aglow, and for one split second Rachel understood what it was to look upon the face of an angel. But it was this same angel that buried the key to the world's death — her father's death — and Rachel's fascination quickly dwindled. Trying to suppress the emotions that were rising deep within her heart, she shook her head in disagreement. Her voice cracked in reply, "No. You are wrong."

At Rachel's protest, Gabriel cocked her head to the side. As she continued her retort, Rachel's voice became stronger. "You are wrong. I'm nothing like the people in these paintings. I'm not extraordinary..."

"You are a lover of languages, are you not?"

Rachel was taken off-guard by Gabriel's knowledge of her profession. "Yes."

"And you have listened to the voice of your calling. Your father sent you the scroll that spoke of my trumpet. You, the beacon of light in your father's darkness. Your father knew that you would figure out the message of the scroll because you do what you love and it was the only way the two of you could communicate. A blessing in disguise, wouldn't you agree? It helped your father find his way again."

"But, I'm not extraordinary...I'm..."

Gabriel advanced upon her, closing the distance with two powerful strides. The look on Gabriel's face was one of pure fury. "DO NOT SAY IT! DO NOT GIVE LIFE TO THAT WORD! YOU ARE A GIFT! CREATED FOR A SINGLE PURPOSE FROM THE MOMENT YOU WERE BORN UNTIL YOUR BODY BREATHES ITS LAST BREATH! *KNOW THY PURPOSE!*" Gabriel was so furious, she looked as if she were about to attack.

"*GABRIEL!*"

Gabriel snapped her head around at the sound of Raphael's voice. Meeting his eyes, she calmed herself.

"*Peace.*"

Gabriel lowered her head. "Forgive me, my friend. I find that I have no tolerance for such language as of late."

Michael continued to watch Gabriel, absorbing all of her actions. She caught him doing so. Gabriel quickly turned away and looked back at Rachel, her voice pleading, "You are not *nothing*! Your life has meaning, Rachel — a purpose. Your existence is marked on the timeline of history should you choose to embrace that purpose. For you are a mirror of the Most High God! You are His message, a verse on the page of His glorious plan. And He is waiting...waiting for you to light your soul on fire over the darkness so that your mantra, your life, is etched into the history of time." She was breathing rapidly. "Never think upon nothingness or emptiness again." Her eyes ignited in flame, *"For the fallen one…he…hears…you…"*

Rachel backed away from Gabriel, but Gabriel moved in on her, *"Your purpose!"* Gabriel's voice was filled with panic. "You must know it! I know you do! For that is what makes you extraordinary in this dying world! You have to know it or it will all be for nothing!"

Rachel shouted back at her in fear, "What do you mean, *my* purpose?!? This has nothing to do with me!" Angry that Gabriel was angry with her, she cried out in self-defense, *"You're* the one who buried your trumpet, not me! *You* were the one who started this all. I don't care if you're an angel or not! My purpose, if there is one, is not to fix your mistake!"

"It has everything to do with you!"

"I would *never* help the devil! That seems to be *your* purpose for doing what you've done! You've helped him before!"

Raphael's eyes grew wide. Michael swiftly moved between Rachel and Gabriel attempting to avoid an attack by Gabriel — for she always attacked. But Gabriel did not move. Instead, she looked like a wave of sorrow had just crashed down upon her.

Her shoulders dropped another inch; another feather fell from her wing. The look on her face was one that Michael had not seen in over a billion years. As angry and frustrated as he was with Gabriel, that look pierced Michael's heart and cut him to the core. It was the same look she had on her face from that once faded memory long ago. For a moment, he had a moment of hope. That the thoughts he had been thinking were not true; that the answer he was seeking would pour forth from her lips. But she said nothing and his hope dwindled into doubt once again.

Screams were suddenly heard from outside the chapel. Raphael's face fell. "Oh no." He and Michael raced outside. Rachel looked at Gabriel one last time before following the male archangels out onto the street.

Gabriel was alone.

"Your purpose…you have meaning here. You all do." Tears stung her eyes as she looked up at the frescoes once more. "She must know or it is all for naught."

It was then that the cold wind blew through the chapel. The melodious, seductive voice called to her once more, *"Gabriel..."*

Gabriel closed her eyes and whispered to the wind, "Not yet..."

The wind swirled up like a tornado and barreled through the chapel doors. She opened her eyes and walked outside.

PLAGUES

Gabriel stepped outside the chapel. Civilians and tourists were screaming in terror as they stared up at the sky. She followed their gaze. Her eyes narrowed the moment she saw it. The stars were disappearing one by one, as if an invisible hand were erasing them from existence with a single sweep.

Another plague.

The cries grew louder. Gabriel watched the moon slowly dim — a shadow covered a third of it, staining it as if spray-painted black. Gabriel sensed Michael's eyes on her and turned her gaze to meet his. He looked at her accusingly as the cries from the crowd echoed in the square. She looked away, unable to meet his stare.

Rachel, in the midst of the panicked crowd, searched for Raphael. She barreled through the throng of bodies until she reached him. "Raphael! Raphael!" She grabbed onto him. He pulled her through the crowd until they were safely standing next to Michael. "How is this happening? My father is dead!"

"Satan only needed your father to play the first tune."

Michael leveled his eyes at Gabriel. "He watches you — *always.*"

Gabriel did not look at Michael. She did not even blink. Instead, she had a far-off look as she spoke, "I buried my trumpet. Neither it nor the ark could be touched by any other angel — except for me — until the first tune had been played. It is all true. Satan needed a human for that purpose alone. If any angel dared touch the ark or my trumpet before the first tune was played, that angel would be cast into the Lake of Fire in hell."

Michael questioned her, "And then what?"

"Once the first tune was played, the spell — so to speak — would be broken and the devil himself could play the remainder of the tunes if he so wished."

"If he so wished!"

Raphael and Rachel walked toward them. Raphael was stunned, "Why would you do this?"

Gabriel's voice fell into panic. "I never thought anyone would do it! To call upon the name of the devil to guide them to it would mean a human would willingly place their soul on a platter and deliver it into the inferno."

Rachel chimed in, "You should have known it was possible. If my father hadn't done it, the antichrist would have."

"The antichrist is a child born from hell. There is no victory in it if it were he. He has no soul to offer."

"And yet you risked a window of opportunity for hell to crash through." Michael crossed his arms over his massive chest as he looked down at her.

Gabriel finally met his glare in utter defiance. "Yes, Michael, I did." She waited for him to continue baiting her, but he said nothing more. Rachel was aghast. "What kind of angel are you?"

Gabriel leveled her eyes at her, "Would my answer matter to you, Rachel Julia Devereaux? Has it ever mattered to you…the kind of angel I am?"

Rachel did not reply.

Gabriel turned away from them. Raphael placed his hand on Rachel's shoulder. Rachel looked at Michael. "Do you know why my father did this?"

Michael lowered his guard as he looked into her wondering eyes. "Yes. Your father wanted to hurt *our* Father — to bring him the same kind of pain and suffering your father experienced every day since your mother died."

Rachel nodded in understanding. "And who better than the Devil to bring suffering and pain to God."

"Yes. He believed the one way to do it would be to bring the devil's reign upon the earth faster so that he can destroy everything my Father set into motion from the first day of its creation to its last." Michael watched Gabriel's face the entire time he spoke. "Little did he know, that *every* pain and suffering his children endure, makes my Father weep." With each word he uttered, he watched for any sign of remorse, any clue or sign that she was still the archangel he had always known her to be. But she revealed nothing.

As she stood on the blood-covered street lost in the thoughts she had yet to reveal, the cold wind blew. It swirled around her like a lover's caress as she stared up at the faded moon. Two more feathers fell from her wings. The wind blew them away and whispered to her once again, *"Gabriel..."*

Raphael and Rachel did not hear the voice...*but Michael did.* His body immediately reacted to that melodious sound. Instinctively he reached for his sword and ripped it from its sheath. His eyes ignited in fiery green flame. He whirled around in Gabriel direction, but she vaulted into the sky, flying on the wings of the cold wind as it moved with her. Michael shouted after her, *"Gabriel!"* His wings exploded from his back. He was about to launch into the sky after her when Raphael stopped him.

"Michael, what's going on?"

Michael continued to watch Gabriel in flight, following her path with his steely eyes. "Gabriel is on the brink of falling from the light."

"Fall? *Gabriel?* Never!"

Michael suddenly spun around. His eyes bored into Raphael's. "Look at me and tell me that the moment you stepped into the chapel and laid eyes on her that the past did not come back to haunt you...I saw your face."

Raphael was shaken by the truth of his words. "No...you're wrong. She is the fiercest amongst us — second only to you. Gabriel was named for the 'strength of God.' She will never fall. She did not fall — not that day and not this one!"

"Believe what you will, Raphael, but I remember a time long ago when you didn't see the same thing coming."

"Where are you going?"

"I'm not letting her out of my sight." He rose into the air. "Meet me at the cave by the northern cliff. You know of which I speak."

Raphael pounded his fist into his chest in salute. Michael soared into the sky after Gabriel. Raphael was left standing there, shaken. He lowered his head whispering to himself, *"It's not possible."* Rachel grabbed his enormous hand. He squeezed it. The moment he lifted his head, his entire body froze. He turned toward the square.

"What is it, Raphael?"

"We're being watched. We need to go." He scooped Rachel into his arms and leapt into the air.

From the shadows of the square, a burnt hand covered in ash reached down and picked up one of Gabriel's fallen feathers. The being clutched it in his hand and slid back into the darkness.

*   *   *

Michael drifted high above the city, scouring the faces of the people below, searching for the archangel with the raven hair. Michael spotted Gabriel perched on the rooftop of a nearby cathedral. She was clinging to the steeple like a suicide ready to jump.

Looking at the wretched state his second in command was in, the sleeping memory opened its eyes once again. He remembered it. He remembered it all. And in the remembering he saw them: Gabriel and Lucifer. How she loved Lucifer and he, her.

Michael could still hear their laughter resonating throughout the seven realms of the heavens. There was nothing she would ask Lucifer that he would not do…all things but one — and the path of that result gripped his chest like a vice, squeezing it tighter and tighter until he could barely breathe. Her broken wings, her battered face, her still body, her silenced voice, a river of blood — the horrors of the past haunted Michael once again.

As the memory resurrected itself, Michael remained in agony as to what to truly believe, for Gabriel had yet to utter a single word that would shed light into what her actions meant and what her thoughts conveyed.

Michael landed softly on a rooftop nearby. He looked across them and over at Gabriel. He studied her face. Even from this distance, Michael could see her masked expression hidden in the shadow of her mind as she looked down upon the emergency camp below as the people milled about in a wave of panic and fear. Her face, so apathetic, so numb, was horrifying to him as she looked upon the souls of mankind in the camp below.

Michael followed her gaze to see what she saw: lost sheep without a shepherd. A sight such as this one enraged Michael to no end for it meant only one thing — *Lucifer was winning.*

Seeing the herd of people down below, Michael could see in their eyes that panicked look of terror — the one that said, "I have only just now realized that I was truly alive, not merely existing. And I want to live now that I have awakened to the realization…I don't want to die." Michael searched the sea of faces of the recently revived beings who had finally understood that death comes for us all with or without our anticipation of it. He saw their eyes turn inward upon their own private thoughts as they weighed their next moments to where the next chapter in life may lead. And he saw their eyes light up in hope the moment General Dante Carter came into view.

Reporters followed Carter around as he weaved his way through the emergency camp. They were filming every single move he made, broadcasting it for the world to see. Carter moved through the camp like water, speaking words of encouragement — to the injured, to those under his command, to those in his way. And with every person he passed came a different language; for this man named Carter was highly educated and could speak in many tongues.

Michael watched as the newly risen shepherd of lost sheep was greeted with smiles, salutes, and hands that reached out to him to touch him, to understand him, to hold onto him with the hopes of never letting go. For the sight of Carter in this city was the only sign of hope these people had seen since the hail rained down and the sky faded to black.

Michael shifted his gaze from the pasture down below and over to Gabriel. She too had narrowed her vision focusing solely on Carter as he moved through the camp. Even from the forlorn state she appeared to be in, Michael caught it — that flicker of change across Gabriel's face as she watched Carter. A small spark of fire ignited behind her eyes. It was that fire within her that had always given Michael confidence in every command he had ever given her. It was her passion for doing God's will that he had always been able to count on. And as fast as the fire emerged, the spark of fury was suddenly gone. All that was left was that haunted look with buried emotion. That was when the doubt settled in and the anger raged in Michael's heart once more.

Michael knew full well that he needed only ask her the one question that tormented his very core, but he could not, for what if what he feared was true? What if Gabriel had turned her back on God and was reaching out to help Lucifer once more?

Humans are not worthy of their creation, he said. *Angels should never be commanded to serve them or help them,* he roared. *Humans should all die so that their tainted souls never set foot in the kingdom of heaven,* he raged.

Looking out at the camp below, Michael could feel the shadow of hell in the mist, but the shadow was not everywhere. There was light amongst the darkness, for there were those that were worthy. Michael could see the tiny few in the sea of black down below. She must see them too.

As if reading his thoughts, Gabriel turned her gaze toward Michael, but she was not looking at him but past him. She was looking out toward the sea. Michael slowly stood and followed her look out onto the Mediterranean. He could see a vacant beach void of any tide rolling in.

No waves.

Alarm slammed into his chest. Michael vaulted into the sky. Gabriel was suddenly at his side. Seeing her beside him, he struggled with what to believe. He made a decision.

"Call to the others." Michael stormed down toward the sea below.

Gabriel rocketed into the sky, hovering high above the clouds. With a thunderous voice she shouted to the four ends of the earth calling to the other archangels, *"RAPHAEL! URIEL! RAGUEL! SARIEL! JEREMIEL!"* Her voice rumbled like thunder across the world.

From the northern cliff, Raphael burst forth from the cave having heard Gabriel's call. Rachel, terrified, followed closely behind him. They looked down and saw Michael on the beach below.

"Raphael…" She pointed toward the sea. An enormous wall of water was moving toward the shore. It was a tidal wave large enough to wipe out the entire city.

"Rachel, stay here."

Raphael flew toward his commander. He landed on the beach at the same time as Gabriel. She stood on Michael's right; Raphael was on his left. One by one the other four archangels dropped from the sky without a moment to lose. Michael shouted to the archangels, *"IN A LINE!!!"*

The angels lined up down the coast, each covering an equal distance of beach.

"WINGS!!!"

All seven archangels expanded their massive wings as they faced the water. All archangels were seraphim, and all had six wings apiece. The color of the angels' wings looked like a rainbow down the shore. Uriel's wings were golden — resembling the sun at dawn. Sariel's were as brown as the earth. Jeremiel's wings were an iridescent gray — likened to a black pearl. Raguel's were royal purple of the ancient Praetorian Guard.

Their wings extended the distance of the coast as the tidal wave approached. The people in the emergency camps were unaware of what was about to befall them, for the night sky had grown dark and the people were still running for shelter from the falling hail and fire. They would never see the wave coming.

"WIND!!!"

As one, the archangels flapped their wings in unison. Their pace quickened, and the force of their united stroke created a mighty wind. The wave towered above them as the power from their wings held the wall of water in place like an invisible dam refusing to break.

"FASTER!!!"

The angels beat their wings faster until the wave started to fall back upon itself.

The cold wind returned. It headed straight for Gabriel... *"Come to me, my love..."*

Gabriel swayed at the sound of the voice that sung to her like a lullaby, lulling her to falter. Her wings began to slow.

Gabriel spoke to the wind, "Give me time..."

The cold wind moved on. Gabriel snapped out of her dreamlike state. Her crimson wings pulsed again catching up in speed to the rest.

The tidal wave was forced backwards, collapsing upon itself again and again until the massive wave shattered into smaller ones as they rolled up onto the shore. Gabriel looked down at her feet.

Red.

Michael looked down and saw a school of dead fish all around his feet. His jaw clenched. *Another plague.*

It was Uriel who spoke the prophesized words, "A third of the sea was turned to blood, a third of the living creatures in the sea died."

"Satan isn't wasting any time, is he, Gabriel?"

Uriel heard Michael's question and was alarmed at the mention of the devil. "What is this you speak of, Michael?"

Michael nodded toward Gabriel. "Ask her."

Uriel walked toward her. "Gabriel..." She smiled faintly as he reached out and took her hands in his. She looked deep into his violet eyes, beckoning his understanding without words. He tilted his head to one side as they silently communicated with one another with words heard by none. Uriel's eyes softened. "Ah, beloved..." He looked at her sadly and gently kissed her forehead.

Michael turned away from them as Sariel, Jeremiel, and Raguel approached. They beat their breast in salute to their leader. "Well done, my friends. Return from whence you came. Protect the people at all costs — the same way you have shown yourselves here. These plagues were not meant to happen. Godspeed."

The archangels exploded into the sky and were gone. Uriel approached Michael and pounded his fist into his chest in salute.

"Uriel, return to the south."

Michael started to walk away from Uriel, but Uriel stopped him. "Michael..." Uriel glanced back at Gabriel. "Do not lose faith in her."

Michael dismissed him. "Go."

Uriel nodded in respect to his leader and rose into the sky, flying to the southern ends of the earth. Raphael and Michael were at a distance from Gabriel. It was Raphael's turn to speak. "No matter what she has done, Michael, it can be undone. It's the trumpet we need."

Michael's amber eyes locked onto Raphael's. He was about to speak when the cold wind blew between them knocking them violently apart. The wind collided into Michael, rocketing him back into the bloodied sea. Raphael was thrown to the ground as the wind blew past them, barreling toward Gabriel. Raphael looked up in time to see it moving towards her. *"Gabriel!"*

She turned just as the wind swirled around her like a tornado. Raphael pushed himself up and raced toward her. Gabriel's knees buckled under the wind's force. A blue fire burst forth from the sand behind her. She fought against the wind as it forced her back into the flames.

Raphael dove toward her, colliding into her, tackling her to the ground away from the fire. The wind whipped upward and then dove downward, extinguishing the flames.

Both the wind and the fire were gone.

Raphael looked down at Gabriel's face. Her eyes were closed. He moved the hair away from her beautiful face. He touched her cheek. "Gabriel." Her eyes fluttered open. Raphael laughed nervously. "You know, you and Rachel need to stop doing that. I'm not always going to be around to catch you when you fall."

She looked up at his gray, compassionate eyes. She smiled softly. "You knocked the wind out of me, Raphael." She touched the side of his face.

Tears stung his eyes. "Don't fall, Gabriel. I couldn't bear it."

Her smile slowly faded.

"Gabriel, what's wrong?"

She was about to answer when Michel stepped up beside them. She dropped her hand from Raphael's face. "It's nothing."

She looked up at Michael. He peered down at her willing her to speak instead of continuing on in silence. Yet her silence was her greatest strength for she had kept many secrets; never revealing her missions; never heralding her clandestine plans as she carried God's messages until God himself commanded her to do so — no matter what the cost.

Looking down at her stoic face, Michael begrudged the thought, *Yes, God has chosen his messenger well.*

SHADOWS

"This can't be the way it's supposed to end..." Rachel turned toward Raphael. "How do we get the trumpet back? That's the only way to keep everyone safe from the rest of the plagues. How do we do it?" Rachel waited expectantly for an answer in reply.

Raphael sat beside her in the cave between the northern cliffs of the Mediterranean. A small campfire burned inside the cave giving it a warm glow. Raphael's hand rested under his chin; the elbow of the same arm rested on his knee. He was deep in thought.

Michael stood at the foot of the cave watching Gabriel look out across the sea. He was ready for action, any movement from Gabriel that would beckon the call of the cold wind. He glanced back at Rachel having heard her question.

Raphael stared at the ground beneath him. "Caves...I hate caves. Full of dirt..."

"Raphael!"

He snapped out of it.

"What?"

"The trumpet???"

"Satan has it now."

"So what? Are you telling me that you're just going to hide here in this cave until the last tune is played and the earth destroyed?" She looked over at Michael. He turned his head away from her, focusing back on the female archangel ahead. Rachel, still in disbelief, pursued it further. *"Raphael?"*

"I don't know what you want me to tell you."

"I want you to tell me that you're going to do something!"

"And what would you have me do? Storm into the inferno amongst thousands of fallen angels waiting there only to stand before my sworn enemy and fight the Lord of Hell for the trumpet?"

"Well...yeah."

Raphael looked at the fire. "It's actually what I was thinking." He frowned. "I'm only sitting in this cave because I've been trying to think of a way it can be done. I've never actually been to hell, you know."

She leaned in to him, lowering her voice, "Couldn't you just ask God to give it to you?"

"Just because I ask doesn't mean He'll do it."

"So...you already asked Him then."

He nodded. "Yes, but I believe there is another being He has chosen for this task and it is not Michael, Gabriel or me."

Rachel was not satisfied with this answer. Her whole body wanted to get out of the cave and get the trumpet. Her inner spirit screamed to do it so that the trumpet was safe with God's angels instead of the hands of their foes.

"Why does he allow it?"

"Who?"

"God. The suffering...the pain. He could stop it if he wanted to."

Michael turned his head back to the conversation.

Raphael's gray eyes glowed in the fire-lit cave. "Yes, He could. But what kind of God would he be if He imposed His will forcing all our actions against *our* own? We would be slaves, Rachel." He shook his head. "I would never love Him if He forced me to love him or act without allowing me a deciphering thought in the matter." He looked out at the flickering flames. "I would defy Him, rebel against him...just like children often do." He looked up at her.

"There is something you must understand about God, Rachel. He is the everlasting Father. He is all. And He *loves*…He loves like no other. He mourns like a storm over suffering and pain…because others have wrought it…by a single choice. They said…*yes*. Yes to folly. Yes to anarchy. Yes to hate. They choose to entwine themselves in the vines of shadow and death. And God allows everyone that freedom: to choose the light or fall into darkness. He allows that freedom for me, for my brothers who have fallen from grace. And He allowed it…for his son."

Rachel listened in silence.

"And His son allowed the vengeful cravings of the world to fall upon his shoulders because he understood…they know not what they do. They did not and do not see the bigger picture, the higher plane — that their father ultimately wants them to come home." He looked at her imploringly. "You and I are very much alike, Rachel. We want to wrap our arms around hope and peace — because life is hard when other people's actions affect our own. Even mine. We abhor ugliness, grief, savagery…and we yearn to hold our brothers and sisters accountable for what they've done. We burn for justice. So does God."

"He could still stop it."

"If He did, if He chose to impose His will, you and I would have nothing to do. We would never move or choose or fight for the bigger picture, the higher plane. We would never have a reason or desire to wrap our arms around hope or peace or love — because we would never recognize a life without it, would we, Rachel?"

Rachel did not answer him.

"If your father had never chosen to play the first tune, you would still be sitting in your office studying words to symbols that no longer matter. You would be stuck in the past. Now, you're moving forward with your sights on the future of the world and mankind discussing one of humanity's greatest questions left unanswered with an archangel. Which existence do you prefer?"

"I'm still not satisfied."

"Not everyone is."

She looked into the fire, shaking her head, "It can't end like this. I want tomorrow to come again." Raphael remained silent allowing her to speak. "I haven't done anything with my life. Not really. I've just been...*existing*. Checking off a list of daily tasks. I haven't fulfilled my purpose, Raphael — not yet."

"And what is your purpose?"

"I don't know. Ever since Gabriel asked me — asked me as if I should already know...I feel more lost than ever." She sighed, deeply troubled. "I don't know why I'm here, why any of us are here, but I know I don't want to die without knowing the answer — without doing the thing that is left undone." She laughed softly. "I want to die when I'm an old woman lying in my bed when my purpose in life is fulfilled."

Raphael studied her face. "You remind me of myself. I asked the same question once. My friend Vitor and I debated our existence often — before he fell. We would sit near the Great Waterfall in heaven and ponder our existence. What were we created for? What is it that we are supposed to do? And the answer came, but not the one I saw coming. And yet, that answer — when it finally showed its face — was the greatest turn in my path that could have been constructed. It was one single moment where I waited for a sign from God to guide my way, but nothing came. It wasn't until I simply decided to step forward and make a decision — to simply move — that I found God moving with me. I was waiting for God to show me the answer, but he was waiting for me to go forth so he could show me. You'll have your answer, Rachel, before you die. You just have to choose to move."

"A choice..." Rachel grabbed his hand. "You're right. I know you're right." She was trembling. "But I'm scared."

"What are you afraid of?"

"I'm afraid that when I move, the path will be harder than I think. That I'll make the wrong choice. That I won't recognize that single moment to seize what defines me in this world." Sirens sounded in the distance. She turned her head toward the mechanical wails. "I'm afraid of dying, Raphael."

"Sounds more like you're afraid of living." She did not say a word. "God does not ask everyone to part the Sea of Reeds, bring down a giant or bear the son of my father. Whatever you are meant to do, Rachel, the only reason to fear death is to know where you are going when you die, and it not being the place you want to be. It's up to you to choose which way you're going to go."

Rachel pondered his words. She was suddenly comforted by them. In her comfort, a thought seized her. "Will you do something for me, Raphael?"

"Besides bursting into hell to get the trumpet without a plan? Sure, what?"

"Tell me about the antichrist."

*   *   *

Outside the cave, Gabriel and Michael had heard the entire conversation between Raphael and Rachel. Gabriel was looking out at the sea watching its waves slowly rise and fall.

"He was wrong, you know."

Gabriel leaned against the rock and turned around to face Michael. Michael stepped forward, his arms were folded across his massive chest. She could see the line of his jaw tightening as he clenched his teeth. "Michael, why don't you just ask me what you really want to ask me? *Why did you bury your trumpet, Gabriel?*"

"It's your trumpet. You can do whatever you want with it."

"Then why does it feel like you doubt my decision without even knowing my intent?"

"What do you mean?"

"The simple fact that you've been watching every move I make since you found me in the desert. That steely glare of condemnation you've had in your eyes since then is quite clear." She smiled challengingly. "You don't trust me."

"You're not yourself."

Her smile grew cold. "I'm your second in command, Michael."

"My second in command was a much wiser angel."

"Have I gone dumb without knowing it?"

"Idleness stupefies the brain — it is the devil's playground."

"Aye, that it is…"

Michael continued to stare at her with his unblinking eyes. "Nobody listens to you anymore, do they, Gabriel? You, our Father's messenger, are ignored by the mortals of the earth. Is that why you don't lift a hand to help them anymore — not even children?"

Gabriel said nothing.

"I remember a time when you would crash through Heaven to get to Earth to battle every single demon who dared look at a human with a single turn of their head." Michael looked her up and down. "And look at you now. You don't even have your bow or your sword to fight. What happened to the angel I used to know with that fire in her eyes and that passion in her spirit? One who had an iron will that could never be undone no matter how hot the flame? Because I respected that angel who stood at my side more than the one I see before me now."

Gabriel's breath quickened at his words. She looked at him challengingly. "Why crash through heaven to get to an earth that doesn't care if I come or not? I lost hope for the humans long ago, Michael. That's no secret. And God has had no message for me to give but the last one."

She turned from him and looked out at the bloodied sea. "I despise the things that I see in this world. I hate them for what they are, for how they came to be. And I can't wait until it is obliterated from my sight, so it can all start anew."

Michael jumped down from the cliff and stormed toward her. "There are still those on earth who didn't contribute to it. They're just caught up in it."

"I know that."

"And our duty is to protect them with everything we have within ourselves, just as you would've done long ago."

She turned toward him. Her eyes steeled. "And what makes you think I haven't?"

"Look at you!"

"Yes, look at me, Michael! See the angel before you that was and is, and judge me not, for you do not know my mind!"

He pointed to her chest. "I don't need to know your mind for I see that your heart is weak."

She erupted at his insult, smacking his hand away, "Never speak to me of weakness!"

"You've been weak since the Crucifixion. That is when it changed. I saw how it changed you."

"Oh, you *saw*. But you are not me and you were not there! You weren't there in Gethsemane with him, comforting him in the garden! You weren't there on the hill that day waiting on his every breath to call upon you to strike down the ones who nailed him to that tree! Men put him there. *Men* — whom God commands me to serve, commands that I stand by their side without judgment in all their folly. *And I obey*. Yes, it changed me — it changed everything! And yet...I still serve with everything I have within me! Don't you ever mistake my humility before God for weakness!"

"Your last great message has been to herald death. Look around you, Gabriel! You speak of humility before God when you gave the key to heaven's gate to the devil! Was that in direct obedience to God's will for the people? To bring them death sooner than it was supposed to happen?"

"You are not my judge! Leave that and me to the Father." Collecting herself she turned toward the edge of the cliff. Dead carcasses continued to float up onto the shore below.

"You know, Gabriel, you talk like him. Even *he* didn't want to serve."

She was about to respond, but held the words deep inside.

"You even look like him when he turned away from God."

"I'm quite tired of this, Michael."

"So was he when he chose to overthrow God. Even then you

tried to help him — you two always helped each other in time of need." Michael grabbed hold of her shoulders and spun her around. He couldn't take it any longer — the question erupted from deep inside, "Are you helping him!" She threw his hands off her. He grabbed her again. "Is that why you buried the trumpet? For *him* to find? For *him* to use?" He picked her up and slammed her against the rock. Gabriel, equally angered, kicked both of her heels into his abdomen, knocking him backward and into the cliff opposite her.

Enraged, he barreled toward her and tackled her into the rocks behind her. The cliff vibrated upon impact. As he rose from the ground, Michael picked her up by her shirt and dangled her in the air. *"WHY! WHY DID YOU DO IT, GABRIEL!"*

Gabriel met his gaze. "For *Him*…"

Michael was so horrified by her answer that he exploded in anger and slammed Gabriel's body to the ground. The force of her impact shook the rock to its core.

*   *   *

Rachel and Raphael felt the quake inside the cave. They heard Michael yelling. Raphael's face fell. "Not again…" They rushed outside.

*   *   *

Michael released Gabriel. Trying to catch her breath, Gabriel rolled to her side away from him. She lay there on the edge of the cliff, her body in pain. She attempted to push herself up but could not find the strength. She fell back down.

Rachel and Raphael saw Gabriel on the ground, battered and dirtied. Michael was standing over her. "You are about to fall, Gabriel. And I will not catch you when you do."

Michael turned his back on her and walked slowly toward the cave. Raphael was bowled over at the scene before him and how it

119

was playing itself out. Michael did not even bother to meet his eye as he passed him.

Gabriel made one last valiant effort to rise. She pushed herself up to standing when the cold wind returned. It swirled around her. Without the strength to fight against it, she was caught in its pull and wake. The wind whipped around Gabriel, rising up and taking the shape of a hand. The hand smashed down upon the ledge, pulling Gabriel down in its grasp. In the blink of an eye, the cliff and Gabriel were gone.

Raphael shouted, *"GABRIEL!!!"*

Michael whirled around faster than Raphael could move. Seeing that the cliff was gone, his six emerald wings shot out as he dove down the slope of the cliff willing himself to fly faster to catch her before she smashed into the rocks below.

He was too late.

A sea of rubble was all that lay before him. Unable to see her body, Michael was beside himself at what had just transpired. The things he said to her. The fight he had with her. Frantically and determinedly, he careened the rocks into the bloodied sea.

Raphael swooped down to join him. "I see her hand!"

Gabriel's hand was sinking amongst the rubble. They moved more rocks until more of her body was recovered. Michael looked down at her unconscious body and was overcome — history repeating itself — but this time *he* was the cause. The wind continued to swirl all around her body, pulling it down.

Michael took his adamantine sword and impaled the wind-like hand. It released its hold on Gabriel. The wind shot up into the surrounding sky and was gone. Raphael quickly knelt down and scooped up Gabriel's body. Raphael looked down at the slashes across Gabriel's face. He turned on Michael, accusingly, "What happened?"

Michael could barely find the words, "I was angry, Raphael." He rubbed his temples, his eyes scrunched together.

"Don't you see? This is what he does. He stirs up fear and pain in order to divide and conquer. Why were you fighting?"

"I asked her why she had done it — why she buried her trumpet. She said…she buried it for him."

"For *him?* For God or for Satan? Which one, Michael? Who did she mean?"

Michael looked lost. "I don't know. I thought…"

Raphael extended his sapphire wings before Michael could finish his thought. Raphael rose to the cliff above, holding Gabriel's body close to him. He landed next to Rachel. She followed him inside the cave.

Michael was left alone on the rocks below, the bloody water rolling against his feet. Seeing Gabriel lying on the rocks had brought on the nightmare of finding her lifeless body once before. The torment of that memory combined with his present action toward her filled him with torment. And yet…he still did not know what to believe. He thought she meant Satan, but Raphael's question…he didn't know who she meant! Michael's heart had been stabbed with a dagger of anguish, wanting to believe she meant God, angry that he didn't think she did. "Father, what is her purpose?"

A seagull floated dead in a pool of water beside him. A large insect buzzed around it. Michael narrowed his eyes zeroing in on the insect. He lifted his eyes to the darkened moon. *"Apollyon."*

APOLLYON

Michael stormed inside the cave. "The Destroyer is here."

Raphael took in the announcement. He shook his head. "The plagues are out of order, Michael. This isn't the next one."

Michael looked down at Gabriel's unconscious body. "They've been out of order, Raphael. Satan is purposely playing them that way so we don't know which will come next — so we cannot prepare."

"We need Gabriel, Michael."

"We're going to have to do it without her."

Raphael's face turned gray. A large insect flew into the cave zooming around Rachel's head. She swatted it away, but another one suddenly zoomed inside, followed by another. Rachel smacked another one. It slammed into the rock wall and fell onto its back. Its legs were curled up in the air — unmoving. Rachel leaned in to get a closer look at it. "This looks like a locust."

The insect suddenly twitched and flipped over. Rachel cried out in surprise. The locust rubbed its front legs together. It fluttered its wings and rose into the air, hovering inches from Rachel's face. It stared at her with large, black, glassy eyes. Its eyes roamed up and down Rachel's face taking in her features as if deciding upon something. The intelligent look it emitted had a human-like quality to it. It gave Rachel the creeps. "What kind of locust is this?"

There was a golden hue around the locust's head. Its silver body shone like a breastplate of armor on a horse prepared for battle. As the insect continued to hover, it batted its wings like a humming bird. But instead of a hum, the sound of its wings was like a stampede of horses across a desert plain. Combined with the sound of the horde of locusts hammering outside the cave, Rachel's question was drowned out. She repeated the question with a shout as her panic set in, "WHAT KIND OF LOCUST IS THIS!"

At the sound of her cry, the locust swung its tail up as if to strike her in the face. Its tail resembled that of a scorpion. Rachel crab-walked backwards away from the insect as fast as her hands and feet could carry her. She watched as the locust zoomed out of the cave to join the rest of the swarm outside. The other two locusts followed suit. "What the hell was that!"

"Another plague." Raphael turned toward Michael. "I'm not prepared to fight a bunch of stinging insects. What's your plan?"

Michael had the most serious look Rachel had seen on his face all night. "We stop Apollyon."

Raphael's face turned from gray to stark white. "We cannot stop him!"

Michael whirled around. "We don't have the trumpet! There is nothing we can do to reverse this without it! We have to stop Apollyon from unleashing the entire nest of locusts upon the earth before they attack everyone everywhere! It's the only way…unless you have a better idea."

Raphael paused. "Coming up empty here." He turned to Rachel. "Watch over her."

Rachel looked at Gabriel's unconscious form. "I think we'll both be fine as long as she's unconscious. But what should I do if more bugs come in here?"

"Not to worry. They only have the power to attack like scorpions. They won't kill you; just torture you with their stings."

"*Torture?!?*"

He stopped. Seeing the look of terror on Rachel's face, he sought to give her words of comfort. "Um, I mean…not you, Rachel. Just everyone else."

He coughed nervously and exited the cave.

Michael stared at Gabriel's wounded form. He knelt down next to her still body and whispered something in her ear. Rachel tried to make it out but could not understand the angelic language.

Raphael shouted from outside the cave, *"MICHAEL!"*

Michael rose and exited the cave. Rachel looked down at Gabriel's sleeping face. She could still hear the archangel's voice summoning the awakening of her soul, *"What is your purpose! You must know it!"*

She leaned in to Gabriel and, like Michael, whispered to her, "What is my purpose, Gabriel? What is it that I'm supposed to do?" As if in reply, the relentless cold wind blew throughout the cave. It swirled around Rachel and Gabriel, pushing between them until Rachel was pinned against the rock wall.

"Come now, beloved."

The fire in the cave turned from orange to blue.

*   *   *

Michael and Raphael stood at the edge of the cliff — or what was left of it. They watched the waves in the sea rise and fall.

"Michael, you're going to have to help me out here. How are we going to fight him? What's the plan?"

"We're going to talk to him."

Raphael silently waited for Michael to continue. When he did not, and he realized that was Michael's plan, he replied, "Oh, yes…a battle of words. Good one."

"Not just a battle of words, Raphael — good old-fashioned reasoning. We shall appeal to his senses."

Michael flew out to the middle of the sea amidst a battalion of locusts. He hovered there and lowered his head in silent prayer to the Father. He took a deep breath and roared the name of the destroyer, *"APOLLYON!!!"* Michael's voice plunged into the waters below him, drowning out the riot of the insects.

Raphael drifted in the sky nearby.

As the waves rose higher and higher, deep within the water, the sea began to moan. The moaning grew louder and louder as the waves continued to rise. A horde of locusts dove toward the direction of the city and headed straight for the emergency camp. Raphael watched them go. *"MICHAEL!"*

Michael could see the horde. He called to the angel of the abyss once again. *"APOLLYON!!!"*

The moaning gave rise to the voice of the destroyer. *"Michael…"*
"APOLLYON! SHOW YOURSELF!"

The waves rose higher and higher joining together into one massive form. A large wave in mid-roll stopped before crashing down. The water continued to roll within itself, funneling an invisible energy, as the wave began to take shape.

Standing his ground, Michael continued to hover in front of the giant wave. The water rolled and flowed, rising until it towered over Michael. The waves continued to shift until the outline of a large beast came forth from within the water…and the destroyer emerged. His body mirrored that of the Titan — the Cracken.

Apollyon had eight massive arms that resembled an insect's legs; his body was that of a large locust; his face was the same as the ones on each of the horde's faces. But instead of being made of solid matter, he was a body of pure water. He was eye to eye with Michael. Apollyon's eye, however, was bigger than Michael's entire body. *"Out of my way, Prince of Angels."*

"Apollyon! Hear me! This is not your time! Call off the locusts!"

Apollyon laughed long and deep.

Michael continued to yell his command, *"CALL THEM OFF!!!"*

Apollyon heaved an enormous mouthful of locusts at Michael in reply. Michael spun around; his wings acted as his shield to protect him from attack as the locusts hammered against them. The insects collided into Michael's wings only to career off of them and into the sky to fly past him and down toward the city. The vicious attack on

Michael continued. He called out, *"RAPHAEL!"*

Raphael raced toward Michael like a bolt of lightning. He spun rapidly as he reached the horde, moving high and low like a steamroller all around Michael. He thwarted the locusts' path by using his body to bat them away from his commander. All the while, Michael moved his body backward, barreling the horde back into Apollyon's mouth. Apollyon was overcome. His body fell back down into the sea.

Raphael stopped spinning. The sea appeared calm as Raphael flew to Michael. They looked down at the sea as it rose and fell. "That wasn't so bad."

Apollyon suddenly exploded up from the deep, looming over the archangels, rising higher than he did before.

"Sorry. Spoke too soon there."

Apollyon took a deep breath and was about to heave another mouthful of locusts at Michael and Raphael when Michael ordered, *"CRISSCROSS!"*

Michael and Raphael dove all around Apollyon's mouth using their wings as nets to catch the locusts as they burst forth. The archangels flew in dizzying fashion, faster and faster, as they used their wings to hammer the horde back down upon Apollyon. They bore down on the destroyer with all their might while Apollyon fought his way upward. Water and locusts exploded in all directions. Michael shouted through the stream of water and bugs, *"APOLLYON, LISTEN TO ME! IT WAS NOT GABRIEL WHO HERALDED YOU! IT WAS SATAN!"*

At the sound of Satan's name, Apollyon roared. Michael continued to shout, *"CALL THEM OFF!"*

Silence.

Michael and Raphael stopped flying and looked all around. The locusts surrounded them, but instead of flapping their wings like a stampede of roaming buffalo, they merely floated in midair like petrified pixies. They stared at the archangels with their human-like faces and black, glassy eyes. Apollyon looked from Michael to

Raphael. *"Where is the archangel Gabriel?"*

It was Raphael who answered, "She's badly hurt. Look to the earth, Apollyon. See with your own eyes how God's angels are trying to stop the locusts from attacking the mortals."

Apollyon weighed his words but did not respond. Michael and Raphael hovered in the air for what seemed like an eternity when the destroyer suddenly rushed forward, colliding into Michael and Raphael, knocking them down into the sea. Apollyon rode the waves to shore; his army of locusts flew with him. He whispered to them, *"Show me..."*

The swarm moved in toward the city. Through their eyes Apollyon could see all that they saw: more of his horde diving in, out, and all around the people in the city as they tried to sting and attack those of their choosing. But with each attempt came failure, for they were barricaded by an invisible field that kept them at bay. Apollyon whispered again, *"Show me the unseen..."*

The locusts hummed in unison as the invisible field dissolved. All around each and every human being was a guardian angel. And with each angel came the protection from the hand of God that would not allow the locusts to bite. Thousands upon thousands of guardian angels shielded their human assignments thwarting off the locusts, protecting young and old alike with their shields, their wings, their sheer will.

The people whom they guarded ducked, flinched, screamed and cried over an attack that never came. Had Michael's words been false, this scene could not be. There would have been no guardians for the mortal men, women, and children of the earth, for it was prophesized long ago that it would not be.

The locusts continued to hum as they showed the fallen angels amidst the unseen shadows. Apollyon could see Gokor, Asmodeus, Nero and thousands of fallen angels shrouded in the shadows of the darkened city. He watched them lust for the violence that the locusts brought but could not deliver. Their drool and cackled snarls grew more frenzied as they watched the guardians drive off the attacks time and time again. The sight of the fallen ones enraged Apollyon to no end. The waves projected his emotion as they crashed faster and faster upon the shore. He groaned the word, *"SATAN!"*

From above, Michael gave the command, *"INTO THE SEA!"*

Apollyon reared his head upward to see Michael, Raphael and twenty warrior angels hovering above him. They dove down into the sea like birds in V-formation. They swam head to toe in a circle until the pull from their motion created a whirlpool. The force from the pool was enough to drag Apollyon back toward the sea. His form diminished wave by wave as the water was pulled out from under him. He could not and did not fight against it.

"CALL TO THEM, APOLLYON!"

Apollyon threw his eight gigantic arms out in front of him; the mist from his powerful limbs fell upon the city. With outstretched arms, Apollyon called to his army with a deep, mournful moan. The locusts rose as one and zoomed back toward their master of the deep. They barreled into Apollyon's arms as he wrapped his eight massive arms around them in a loving embrace.

The angels swam faster. Apollyon and his brood continued to be pulled down into the abyss by the force of the angels' momentum. Michael shouted to his angels, *"PULL UP!"*

The angels vaulted into the sky before they too were sucked down. Apollyon was dragged down into the whirlpool, and his body dissolved back into the sea. The waves died down and the sea was calm once more.

Michael and the rest of the angels hovered a little longer to ensure that no further sign of Apollyon existed. Satisfied with his exit, the twenty warrior angels pounded their chests in unison to Michael. They vanished. Only Raphael and Michael were left drifting in the sky.

"I never liked that Apollyon."

"He was doing what he was created for, Raphael. And he will do it again. Only next time we won't stop him."

"It would have been a lot easier if we had the trumpet. Gabriel could have played the tune that would have reversed the plague."

"RAPHAEL!"

They heard Rachel screaming from the cave. The archangels looked toward it and saw a blue light glowing from inside. The shadow of a hunched creature flickered against the rock wall.

"Felix." Raphael dove down.

*　　　*　　　*

Rachel was holding onto Gabriel's body with all the strength she had within her. Her arms were hooked underneath Gabriel's. She pulled Gabriel's body toward her, screaming as she tried to hang on. Felix was at the other end of the cave. He was on his stomach; his claw pulled at Gabriel's foot as he attempted to drag her body back toward the shadows of the cave from whence he came. With the use of his stunted arm, he swatted at Rachel, trying to get her to release her hold. Rachel kicked at Felix's nub; he roared in pain. *"Get away from her!"* Felix tugged harder. Rachel's grip loosened.

Raphael was in the cave. He lunged for Gabriel's wrists just as Rachel completely lost her grip. Raphael pulled Gabriel back toward him gaining the better ground. Felix snarled and another fallen angel slithered forth on his belly from the shadows of the cave — *Azriel.*

Azriel locked his burnt, distorted fingers onto Gabriel's calves and pulled. It was a tug-of-war over Gabriel's body. Her body was slowly slipping from Raphael's grasp. He cried out, *"GABRIEL! FIGHT! DO YOU HEAR ME! FIGHT!"*

Gabriel's eyes snapped open. She saw the fallen ones at her feet. She rolled over as fast as she could, grabbing onto Raphael's shirt. The fallen ones yanked as one and Gabriel's grip was lost on Raphael as his shirt began to tear in her grasp. She slid further down into the shadows. She grabbed onto Raphael's forearms, but she was too weak to hold on. She slipped from Raphael's grasp.

Michael rushed inside.

Rachel moved out of the way as Michael lunged for Gabriel's

arms. Raphael and Michael pulled Gabriel toward them with equal counterforce as the fallen ones pulled at her feet. Gabriel screamed in pain as her body was torn in two. She locked eyes with Michael. *"LET…GO!"*

"NO!"

Raphael shouted at her, *"NO, GABRIEL!"*

She screamed in agony as Felix dug his claw into her leg. *"LET GO!"*

Michael's amber eyes bore into hers, *"NO!"*

Gabriel's voice was monstrous in reply; it thundered inside the cave as she shouted, *"I AM YOUR SECOND IN COMMAND, MICHAEL!"* She stared deep into his eyes willing him to see what lay within. With barely a sound, she whispered, "*Let go…*"

And Michael did.

He ripped Raphael's hands free from her body. Raphael tried to fight him, but was overpowered by Michael's iron will. Raphael cried out, *"NO!!!"*

He watched in horror as she was dragged into the shadows at the hands of the fallen angels. Gabriel's face never left Michael's. And then…she was gone.

Raphael scrambled forward in an attempt to grab hold of her hands but it was all in vain. The doorway from whence the fallen ones came had closed.

Raphael rammed his body into the rock wall again and again, trying to break through, willing the shadowed doors to open for him. In utter despair he wailed, *"GABRIEL!!!"*

Rachel watched him; tears streamed down her face from her adrenaline rush at what had transpired. Her heart hammered at what she had just been a part of and what she had witnessed. She looked at Michael, searching his face to understand what he had just done. It was then that she saw Michael looking at the blue flames still burning in the fire pit.

A laugh emoted from deep within the fire. *"She is ours…ours…ours…for the kingdom…I…I…I…"*

Rachel shuddered in terror, "Where did they take her?"

Michael turned his head toward Rachel, his face was extremely grave. *"Hell."*

The light went out.

HELL

Gabriel lay facedown on the ground. She immediately flipped over and kicked at both Felix and Azriel, but they had suddenly disappeared leaving her all alone. All she could hear was the faintest of whispers, *"The kingdom...the claimant...the master..."*

Gabriel immediately collected herself and pushed herself up to sitting. She looked all around but could barely see through the thick cloud of fog surrounding her. Gabriel attempted to stand but was too weak and lacked the energy to do so. She collapsed against something solid directly behind her. She reached up, feeling its base, but could make nothing out. She rested her head against its firm foundation and closed her eyes. She breathed hard, attempting to calm her mind with slow even breaths.

This was not the hell she remembered. No torches burning through the fog; no rain of fire or ash falling down upon her. Even the sulfurous smell of brimstone was gone. What part of hell was she in? Breathing in long and deep, she could make out the faintest aroma — a pleasant one — almost like...a flower. *But a flower...in hell? Where was it coming from?*

She couldn't even hear the human melodies of mournful song coming from the mortal souls inhabiting the inferno. Where had they all gone? And then she heard them, the faintest sound of footsteps. *Powerful ones.*

The cold wind suddenly blew gently across her face. *Beloved...*

She opened her eyes.

Gabriel saw the golden hair, the broad shoulders, the athletic form as he moved toward her — and it was perfect. The outline of his six enormous wings brushed the fog from his path as he strode confidently though it.

"He is my greatest friend, Michael...before oaths and duties....Come home, Lucifer..."

"Gabriel...I cannot...God will not listen! He will not bend! You have eyes but you do not see!"

The fog moved away and the angel of light, the Morning Star, came forth.

"Hello, Gabriel." A brilliant smile was spread across Lucifer's face. His eyes shone brightly in joy as he drank in her presence.

My friend of old...

They stared at one another. Moments passed before either of them spoke; each took in the other's face. It was Lucifer who moved first. He crouched down to her until their faces were inches apart. His opaque-colored wings retracted into his body. The smile never left his face.

"I have missed you."

Gabriel rested her hand against his well-sculpted jaw. Looking deep into his beautiful blue eyes, a sudden sadness crept into her heart. Her eyes filled with tears. Lucifer's face fell at seeing her sorrow.

"Gabriel, what is it?"

"You look so much like him...the Enlightened One...my friend...you were so beautiful when you stood in the light. How I loved you so. We all did."

He laid his hand on top of hers; his expression was one of angst, "I am still your friend. I will always be that angel you loved so long ago."

She dropped her hand from his face. "No, that time is long forgotten. It will be nevermore."

Lucifer shook his head. "No, you are wrong, my love. I knew you would return to me and now you are here." He smiled sadly, "I have waited *so* long for this moment." He took her hand and held it to his heart. "Seeing you here…makes me…*happy.*"

The moment he placed it there, the fog around Gabriel and Lucifer immediately lifted and the kingdom of the fire world was revealed. Gabriel was stunned at what she saw.

She looked at Lucifer. He smiled proudly at her bewildered reaction.

"Recognize it?"

The fire, smoke, ash and brimstone — they were all gone. As far as the eye could see, a beautiful garden filled its landscapes. Instead of the Lake of Fire, there were waterfalls, brilliant mountains and vibrant trees. Gabriel shifted her gaze from flower to branch to water to stone. The aroma of flowers filled her senses. She breathed in their scent.

She looked behind her to see what she was leaning against and saw that it was a tree — the largest tree in the garden. She ran her hand along the trunk feeling its texture. She rapped her fingers against it. *Real.* Gabriel looked back at Lucifer. He beamed at her with utter joy and satisfaction. His look was absolutely infectious, and it took all of Gabriel's dwindling energy not to look at him and smile back.

"Illusion or creation? How did you do it?"

"Life is what we make of it, is it not?" His eyes roamed the garden. "It's all about perspective. This is mine."

"The Garden of Eden…" She touched the trunk behind her. "And a copycat Tree of Life — nice touch."

Lucifer's smile faded. He looked up at the branches of the tree. "It is more than a copy, Gabriel. It is a monument of remembrance." He looked at her, studying her face. "I have wanted you to see this for quite some time." He paused. "I knew you of all angels would understand my desire for creating this."

He waited for her to say something, but she turned away. "Look at me, Gabriel." He touched her face, gingerly turning it towards him. He took in the scratches on her cheek. His jaw tightened as he ran his finger over them. "This looks like Michael's work." Gabriel pushed his hand away. "Why did he do this to you?"

She looked him dead in the eye, "He didn't do this to me…I fell from a cliff. A lot of unforeseen *wind*."

Lucifer shook his head in amusement. "You're still the same, Gabriel. And yet you look so very different from when I saw you last."

Her lips curled into a smile, "That's because the last time you saw me I was aiming a lightning bolt at your head."

"It wasn't my head you were aiming at, my love."

"Why have you dragged me down here?"

"As if you didn't know." He smiled coyly at her. "To thank you, of course…for giving me your trumpet."

"I didn't give it to you…I *lent* it to you."

Lucifer continued to drink in every feature, line, and curve of her face. "Why you refused to join me so long ago, I will never understand."

"No servant is greater than his Master."

"That is true. I tell that to my servants all the time." Lucifer stood and lent his hand to help Gabriel up. She ignored it and used the last of her strength to push herself up by using the tree as leverage. It hurt her to do so. She winced in pain. Lucifer reached for her to help her, but she smacked his hands away.

"Gabriel, will your stubbornness never wane? Let me help you!"

Defiantly, she forced herself to stand. Lucifer dropped his hands to his sides. Breathing hard, Gabriel turned away from him and looked at the garden.

Such beauty…

Lucifer came up behind her. His silky fingers gently moved her long raven hair away from her shoulders. "Tell me what is wrong, beloved."

She yanked her head from his touch. Gabriel walked forward, but

Lucifer grabbed her shoulders and forced her back against his chest holding her to him. He whispered in her ear, "Are you still angry with me, my love? Angry that I tried to overthrow the Father? For my hating His son? For leaving you?"

She stared straight ahead. "You didn't leave, Satan, you were thrown."

Lucifer spun her around tightening his grip on her. *"Do not speak that name to me!"*

"Do you prefer *'Devil?'"*

His eyes narrowed. "Tell me that you have missed me, Gabriel. I know that you have. Michael, Raphael and the others are hardly sufficient replacements to fill *my* void."

Looking at Lucifer's face, the face of her friend of old, she remembered him the way he was, the way they were. "I missed you once..."

His face softened as the words he had longed to hear were finally spoken. *"Once?"*

"Only once."

Lucifer released her and moved a few feet away. He spit out the word, *"Once."* He bent down and picked up a piece of fruit from the ground. "I miss you all the time, Gabriel...all the time." His voice was filled with longing. "Perdition is not the same without you." Lucifer turned around and looked at her. "You smashed my heart into a thousand pieces."

Gabriel said nothing. He looked down at the fruit in his hand. "It's ironic, you know, that the battlefield of the afterlife began with a single bite from a piece of fruit — a single choice. I often wonder what would have happened if Eve had said no. Or if Adam had refused her offering. I suppose I would have realized at some point that I could have been wrong about humanity. Perhaps I would have looked at the earth and thought there was something from God's creation that I could learn.

"But I don't know what it would have been. Only God's son had something to teach me after he was crucified — that I will never understand God. *Unconditional love.* That I know. I have felt that love, Gabriel — burning in the fire of God's light, standing so close to his heart; it is absolute ecstasy. But God's son…he gives me pause. He revolutionized the idea of forgiveness, in my mind…" He was lost in thought.

"Why the son of God chose to absolve his crucifiers is unfathomable to me. They didn't deserve it. They still don't. And yet, they were redeemed — without even asking for redemption — and they are allowed an eternity in heaven because of it." He looked at her. "What about *me?* Why not extend the idea of forgiveness to *me?* I have killed no one. I am not the one who nailed God's son to a tree. It was never my intention to destroy God — just overthrow him."

He took a bite of the fruit. "I have pondered this idea often: forgiveness. It assumes that some crime has been committed. That somehow, a single action I have chosen was evil and must be absolved so that I may become good once again — pure." He looked out at the landscape around him. "Rebelling against your father is not a crime; it is a challenge of growth. And yet he cast me here. He even forgave Adam and his Eve."

He took another bite of the fruit. "So how is it that I am responsible for all of mankind's undoing — death, illness, wrath, lust, greed, sloth, madness, suffering — when I never forced a single soul to make that choice toward it? I only offered them the fruit — the alternate option to purity, goodness. To show God…he was wrong. Any existence without the presence of God is evil. Humanity…is the all-consuming evidence of wretchedness. It is they who are their own undoing. For God made another mistake…he allowed them choice. And many said yes to the fruit. They said yes against purity. And it is *I* who am suffering for it."

Gabriel remained silent.

"God is perfect. There is no darkness within him. That's what you said." He shook his head. "There is no darkness in me. I only live where it resides, Gabriel."

Lucifer looked out at the landscape once again. "If I am created in the image of the Most High God, I cannot possibly be evil, for I am just like him; it is from God where my pride came from. God is proud. He is too proud, for he does not forgive me because he knows I have been right from the very beginning about his beloved humanity. That is why forgiveness is not for me — whether I ask for it or not. Utter hypocrisy." Lucifer tossed the fruit onto the ground.

Gabriel took in his words. "They asked for forgiveness — whether or not you heard their prayer. And they were given it...because they were actually sorry for what they had done."

The moment she uttered the words, a change came over Lucifer. His face softened as he looked at Gabriel. "Gabriel..."

Gabriel turned away. She stepped into the garden. Lucifer slowly followed. "You've never been sorry." There was a look of anger on her face. *"Not ever."*

Lucifer stopped walking. "Yes, I have. Gabriel, look at me."

She did not turn.

"Please, beloved. Look at me..."

Gabriel lowered her head. After several moments, she slowly turned. She lifted her head and looked at him accusingly. Tears filled his eyes. "I *am* sorry, Gabriel...for what I did *to you.*"

*   *   *

Michael gripped his head in utter torment. Rachel looked over at Raphael. His gray eyes stared accusingly at Michael; they were wild with anger. Before Rachel could stop him, Raphael launched at Michael. She shouted, *"Raphael!"*

Michael looked up in time to see Raphael coming straight toward him. Raphael collided into him, tackling him to the ground. Raphael swung his fists in frenzied emotion. Michael dodged and blocked all his blows while Rachel looked on helplessly. Michael went for Raphael's neck, binding him in a clinch before throwing him off. Raphael looked at Michael with eyes of betrayal. *"You gave her to him!"*

"Raphael! Listen to me!"

He lunged for Michael once again, but he was no match for Michael's skill of battle. Raphael was easily overpowered. Michael forced Raphael down to the ground; his knee was in Raphael's back. Raphael tried to push himself up but failed.

"I'm going to let you up, Raphael, but you have to listen." Michael slowly lifted his knee. Raphael scrambled up, spinning around to face Michael. Michael put his hands out in front of him. "Peace, Raphael. Peace." Raphael's face softened. Michael tried to find the right words. "I let her go…because she said the words, Raphael. She said the words I had long forgotten. She *is* my second in command."

It took Raphael a few moments to understand Michael's meaning. "The *words*, Raphael…"

Raphael slowly nodded; another memory from long ago. Rachel saw the look that passed between the two archangels. She suddenly understood. "The trumpet. She's going to get her trumpet."

Both Michael and Raphael looked at her. A look of pride resided behind Michael's eyes. "God has chosen his messenger well."

*   *   *

Lucifer's eyes bored into Gabriel's. "Forgive me." She remained silent. He moved toward her, kneeling at her feet. Lucifer grabbed hold of her hands and looked up at her with pleading eyes. "I beg you, beloved…forgive me."

She took a deep breath. "Why?"

"As proof that I can be redeemed." He continued on. "Because you are not so proud as to see my side. You have eyes that see, Gabriel. Give me the hope I desire. I need you to."

"You have never needed me before."

"I need you now." He shook his head. "There is no other angel here that knows me the way you do. There is no one here I can talk to. I speak and they obey. No one tests me, challenges me — they simply do. I can't stand it sometimes. They have become what I never wanted to be — a slave. I want to be free of them, Gabriel."

He pulled her closer to him; his eyes were filled with tears. "Say you forgive me, say you believe me."

Gabriel took in his words. "I believe you."

Lucifer smiled sadly. "But not forgiven." He rose from his position and let go of her hands. "I wasn't wrong to do what I did — rebelling against God. I can tell by reading your eyes that you know I speak the truth. All the things that you have seen on the earth, especially the actions of mankind as of late. I know you see the world as I do. Your trumpet was your voice."

Gabriel's face showed not a flicker of emotion. "Speaking of my trumpet, I couldn't help notice how out of practice you were in the musical instrument arena."

His eyes glowed. "How do you mean?"

"You are playing it as if you just learned how."

Their eyes locked. Lucifer smiled. "But it was I who taught you to play."

"And it was you who composed the tunes. One melody for each of the seven realms of heaven. How did you know I would choose those particular tunes to herald the plagues?"

He slowly rose. "*I…know…you.*" He moved closer and reached up to caress her face. "Besides, those were the only tunes you ever learned to play."

She smiled. "You mean…the only tunes you ever taught me." She took his hands in hers and turned them over, gently examining them as she stroked her fingers over their flesh. "Odd then, isn't it? That the master musician in all of heaven would have such a hard time playing his own tunes? Has hell affected the lungs? Singed the fingers?"

He pulled his hands away from her. "Why did Michael attack you?"

"I already told you…I fell."

Lucifer's jaw clenched. "*Before* you fell, Gabriel."

She held his stare. "He thought I was helping you."

A faint smile appeared on the corner of Lucifer's lips. "Fighting over me once again, my love? It seems so long ago when you argued with him over me — protecting me." He touched her face. "You loved me then."

She reached for his hand and lowered it from her face. Gabriel slowly stepped back from him. "Is that why I buried my trumpet? For love of you then? For love of you now, *Lucifer*?"

He moved swiftly toward her, for she had said his name of old. Lucifer grabbed hold of her face in his hands. He touched her lips with his fingers. "Say it again, Gabriel. Say my name, my love. I love the sound of your voice when you say it."

Gabriel looked at the longing in his eyes. "It is not your commands I obey." She threw his hands off her. A fire ignited behind Lucifer's eyes.

"You are still second in command aren't you, Gabriel?"

"Being first in command would mean that I would have to fight you."

"Why not fight me? What is it that you fear?"

"Nothing. God is beside me." She smiled at him challengingly. She looked deep into his ice-blue eyes.

"Still the same, Gabriel…"

At his words, the smile on her face fell into one of anger. "And so are you. You're a fool, Lucifer! You should have listened to me! You should have come home with me! If you had, none of this would be happening! And you would *not* be here!"

"I could not come home, Gabriel! You know I could not!" His voice was stricken. "Not even for you …you left me! You left me in the shadows and the dark! I couldn't let you abandon me! You have no idea what it was like to watch you turn your back on me to fly to the other side of the battlefield to lead an army against me!"

"Don't I? You stand there and look at me as if you are innocent! Do you know who you're talking to! Are you so used to unchallenged action that you think I can be so easily deceived!" She turned her back on him and looked out at the garden before her. "Your claim to innocence reeks of the hypocrisy you accuse our Father of." Her voice fell to a whisper, "Oh, you look so much like him, my friend long past…"

Lucifer moved closer to her, wrapping his arms around her. "I am still your friend, Gabriel. And I am here with you now, my love." He lowered his head onto her shoulder. "Do you remember how it was? How you and I once were together? Finishing each other's thoughts. Sharing our secrets with only each other. Why did you leave me, Gabriel? Why?" Their bodies began to sway to a silent tune. "Stay with me. Never leave me again, my love." He whirled her around; they danced slowly together amidst the garden.

Gabriel rested her head against his. "Do you remember when you asked me to join your side and rule as queen of heaven?"

"Yes."

"Do you remember my reply?"

He sighed deeply. "You said, 'There will be a queen of heaven one day, but it will not be me.'"

"We were made to live in heaven, Lucifer." He held her close. "I am still here in hell with you only because I have not asked God to take me from this place."

He whispered in her ear, "Then never ask him, beloved, for they are words that are daggers to my heart." They continued to sway. Gabriel looked up at him; his eyes bored into her. "*Stay with me…*" His melodious voice from the past echoed in her ears. Gabriel looked into Lucifer's eyes as their bodies swayed as one.

"I saw you that day. And I heard all that you said, Lucifer, all that you wanted. And it was then, standing on a cliff in hell that I missed you — but only once."

Lucifer held her stare. "Then why not ask God to take you from me now if you wish to leave?"

"I need time."

They stopped dancing. Lucifer released her and backed into the tree to lean against it. "Ah, time…" He looked up at the branches and raised his arm to hold onto one directly above his head. "How I have been waiting ever so patiently with my time. And because of you, it is almost near."

Lucifer looked down at Gabriel. "I, too, saw you that day. It was the darkest day of my life and yet you were there. And I thought, for a single moment, that you had followed me here to be with me; to stay with me. That you had forgiven me, seeing that I was right in my argument with our Father. But I saw how you looked at me; and it was then that I understood. You hated me, despised me. I had never seen that look upon your face before, and there it was, and I the cause." He gripped the branch tighter. "And I could not bear it, Gabriel." He ripped the branch down from the tree and hurled it across the garden. It smashed into a rock. He looked back at her with a look of hatred. "I wanted to tear your eyes out so that you could never look at me that way again."

He stared at her for a long time.

"You miss Him, don't you? You miss heaven, God, the light."

The fierce look Lucifer had upon his face softened. "I sometimes miss…the light. But what I miss most…is the *music*. You know I do." He breathed in deeply and closed his eyes, remembering it: the sound, the melody, the voices of song. "The incarnation re-harmonized the symphony of creation. And that is the only melody I hear playing upon the earth over his beloved humanity…*love*…*love*…*love*…how I *hate*…*hate*…*hate*…that tune. It reminds me of the face of God! And I cannot *stand* it! He has wronged me!"

He opened his eyes. "Why do you torment me with images of the past! What do you want from me, Gabriel?"

She waited. "I want my trumpet."

Lucifer's body stilled. "Why?"

"You asked me what I wanted; that is what I want."

He studied her. "All right, on one condition: tell me God's plan; tell me how he is going to try to stop me from playing the final tune."

"He hasn't told me of any new plan."

Lucifer's face was one of stone. "You lie, Gabriel."

Her eyes grew cold. "No, you do. You're the father of them."

He advanced upon her. "Tell me."

"There is no plan, Lucifer. The antichrist's time is near and all that was foretold shall come to pass when the last tune has been played."

"*Tell me*, Gabriel."

Gabriel looked deep into his ice blue eyes and saw that they were darkening. She suddenly looked horrifically sad. Tears filled her sable eyes as her unknown sorrow spread across her face. "The last command that the Father was to give me was to herald the seven plagues of Armageddon when the antichrist came to power. I knew that once I carried out the prophesy, there would be no purpose left for me, the messenger, anymore."

"No purpose in life…what a death."

"When the antichrist was born, so was the idea." She looked off into the confines in her mind.

"Bury the trumpet."

"Yes!" She looked excitedly at Lucifer.

"Bury it for me to find."

She paused. "Or…for no one to find."

Gabriel had Lucifer's full attention. As he stared at her, his hair began to lose its golden hue; it had faded to an ash-blonde. The fog had started to set in on the garden once again. Gabriel had a far-off look as she spoke the words she had held captive within her heart for over forty years; forty years of burden; forty years that had consumed her and eaten away at her until the only audience she had to hear her words was the Lord of Hell. But it was the Lord of Hell for whom these words had been saved and they flowed from Gabriel's mouth like a flood; there was no stopping them.

"I have always had a deep love for the people of the earth — telling myself that you were wrong to hold them accountable for all of the mistakes and choices they had yet to make. I wanted you to be wrong. You had to be wrong. So I warned them, protected them, spoke to them, demanding that they hear my voice and know that there is God. That there is a purpose to it all. That they are not alone, for they have a Father in heaven that loves them like no other. And they listened. They heard because they believed. But it has all changed. They no longer listen. They do not seek to hear. So I stopped talking. And then the antichrist was born and the idea came again — *bury your trumpet*. Bury it to keep it silent."

Lucifer was bothered by her words, unsure of her meaning. "You buried it to help *the people?*"

"I had to fulfill my purpose…" She looked up at him; there was a wild look in her eye. "Don't you see?"

"What purpose, Gabriel?"

"I am The Messenger! And I had none to bring!" She paced back and forth like a caged animal. "I had to bury it! Bury it so I wouldn't be useless! Bury it to help the people…or help…*someone else.*"

She stopped her frantic pacing and sat down against a nearby rock. Her face suddenly changed; her eyes hardened and her face darkened. "Bury it knowing that someone else might be watching me do it; someone who is always watching me; the one who has tried to stop me all these years from carrying out my messages; someone who waits for my descent upon the earth to see whom God has singled out and for what purpose. Bury it for that someone to see."

"Me." He knelt before her. Gabriel looked at him. "Bury it for me to take, to use to abort the world of God's fruitless creation — the way I have always said it should be."

Gabriel touched his face. "Use it by lending it to a fallen friend."

"To help him because he is right in all that he has said and done…"

"…in all that he has wanted from the beginning."

"Rebel against what you have been told — servant to none; ruler of all." Lucifer took her hand from his face and kissed it softly. "Bury it *for me.*"

Gabriel touched his head, combing her fingers through his wavy hair. "To bring my old friend's authority over the Earth faster so that he may call Heaven down to him once and for all? Is that not a purpose?"

Lucifer looked up at her; his face was one of stone. "How I have missed you, Gabriel. I knew you would join me in my argument one day — because I have always known that I was right."

"You claim to know my mind."

"I always did."

"Give me my trumpet."

"You have no need for it, Gabriel."

"I want it."

"I want heaven."

They held each other's stare. "Don't you know your purpose, Lucifer?" Gabriel's eyes suddenly lit afire. "*You will never have heaven.*"

Lucifer's face twisted into one of pure fury. He erupted and struck Gabriel hard across the face. The force of his hand knocked her to the ground. He rose and stood over her; his face began taking on a hue of gray. The fog was now just as thick as it was when Gabriel was first dragged into hell.

Lucifer took in the sight of her form on the ground, relishing it. "Oh, but I will have it. And your trumpet is helping me get it. Look at me, Gabriel."

She did not turn around. Instead he lunged for the back of her hair and wrenched her head up so that she was forced to look at him. "I will give you a new purpose, my love. You will remain here with me in the inferno so that I can do with you as I please. Your screams, beloved, will bring me joy, for you shall never leave me again. That is how I thank all who follow me, all who help me; even you, old friend — for unlike God's son, I forgive *no one.*"

A smile slowly spread across her face. Lucifer looked at her in confusion. "Then you had better thank God." He dropped her head. "But I do not think you will want Him here in hell with you." She rolled over and moved backward on her hands and feet. He followed her slowly, step by step. They could barely see one another through the thickness of the fog.

She spoke again, but this time her voice was filled with utter fury. "For I shall tell you a story…about the Father and his so-called *son*! A son who always believed he knew better than the one who knows all.

Enlightened One he was called — a son who claimed to have loved his Father. An angel who betrayed his Father's love and sought to destroy him. An angel who forgot that the Father knew the truth within that angel's heart. The truth that he sought to hide from all — including the Father. But the Father knew. The Father knew that the argument the angel laid at his feet was not the truth from within — for there was more.

"And so the Father readied himself for what he hoped the angel would not do. And the angel did it anyway. But what that angel forgot was that the Father had *other* sons, *other* angels who would hold their brother accountable. That angel forgot about them and, more important, he thought not on the Father's daughter. For the daughter, too, has eyes! And the daughter loves her Father beyond imagine; a daughter who would do *anything* he asked, for the daughter knows what the angel did not — *I AM...IS ALL!*" She was breathing hard.

"Have you forgotten! Have you forgotten how it ended between you and me! It was *I* who knew you best amongst the angels! Even now, you still do not understand, just as you refused to understand then — *it's not about you!*"

Her eyes narrowed in utter spite. "For there are *other* ways of accomplishing one's goal. When one door closes, another one opens. There is *always* another way. There is always hope. There is always a weakness lurking behind every strength waiting to be torn down. Even you have one. And I have always known it. *Vanity.*" Lucifer seethed as he recognized his words from long ago. "As if I would ever help you unless commanded by the Adonnai to do it. It is His commands alone that I obey! God has always known how you would act because he has always known your heart. 'Bury your trumpet, Gabriel. Bury it where Satan will see you do it. He will take it.'"

"I don't believe you."

"*You* who *never* take your eyes off of me..."

"You are trying to fool me."

"You who claim to know my mind..."

147

The shape of Lucifer's face shifted. Where a chiseled face once was, a wider, more bloated face now resided. The length of his face started to stretch. One of his eyes turned from blue to a fiery red until a serpentine slit formed in the pupil. "*LIAR!* The Father would never allow such a thing!"

"*It was a direct order, Lucifer!*"

"He doesn't work that way!"

Gabriel's face darkened. "You who claim to know the mind of *God?*"

Lucifer suddenly lunged down at Gabriel and picked her up and slammed her hard against the tree. The tree itself had turned black. Its branches so open with offering a moment ago had twisted upon itself to look like a tree of thorns. "You know He doesn't! He hasn't placed his seal on their foreheads for protection. God does not send his sheep to the slaughter at the hands of the Devil!"

"*THEY HAVE THE SEAL!*"

He dropped her, overwhelmed by her revelations. She moved away from him, but he never took his eyes from her. "A life lived for God, in God and of God *is* the seal of God! It was never meant to be literal! From the day their soul is breathed forth into the womb, God's hand is on their heads. For Him to leave his mark, all they need do is choose the father of their own free will and live their lives in honor of that choice. And it would never matter when Armageddon was upon them…because they would be saved!"

Lucifer's skin had lost its luminescence and taken on a scaly, snake-like quality. "Why order it buried!"

They circled one another. Gabriel was on her guard but she was weaponless. "*Time.*"

He stopped dead in his tracks.

"To give them time. Just because you unleashed the plagues early, didn't mean the world was going to end or that your time and that of the antichrist would come any sooner. There is a prophecy of old and it will play through as it was meant to. Unleashing the plagues now, Lucifer, has caused hardened hearts to soften, lost souls to find their way, the blind to see, the lame to walk, and eyes to lift to the kingdom of heaven. Souls that would have been yours had you never had the antichrist play a note on *my* trumpet."

Lucifer's eyes narrowed.

"How dare you give my trumpet to a human without a soul!"

Lucifer was seething.

"Oh, you've been busy on the souls of mankind, but God was not going to let you get so far with so many so fast. For no angel will ever rise above the Father. For we angels are servant to one and the Father rules *all!*"

Lucifer exploded at Gabriel. His body erupted in strength and height. Black, razor-sharp wings jutted out from his body as he roared into hell. Onyx horns protruded from his head. The golden hair and light of Lucifer was gone. All that remained was Satan — the devil himself.

The Garden in Hell vanished to reveal the fire world as it always was: sulfur, ash, and fire. The Tree of Life transformed into a tree of death. Satan charged toward Gabriel; she looked for means of escape but had nowhere to go. She braced herself for the blow. Satan collided into her and pinned her against the tree; his horns trapped her head, caging her in on both sides. He grabbed hold of her neck with his giant fist and squeezed; his one eye was snake-like while the other remained its angelic blue. She was choking, *"You...will...not...win."*

Satan released his hold. Gabriel fell face first on the ground just before his feet. Looking down at her gasping for air, the rage inside Satan continued to build. He threw his horned head back and plunged it down into Gabriel, impaling them into her again and again until it seemed he would never stop. When he finally did, his voice was void of all emotion. "This is only the beginning for you, Gabriel."

Gabriel tried to crawl away; he allowed her to struggle against the pain, watching in amusement as she limped away from him. "Where are you going, beloved?" Satan slithered up behind her; he threw his head back once again and slammed his head down with a final impaling of his horns; they tore through her abdomen. Her screams echoed throughout the inferno.

Satan ripped his horns from her body and roared to the onyx sky of Hell, *"I WILL ASCEND INTO HEAVEN! I WILL EXALT MY THRONE ABOVE THE STARS OF GOD! I WILL SIT UPON THE MOUNT OF THE ANGELIC HOST! I WILL ASCEND ABOVE THE HEIGHTS OF THE CLOUDS! I WILL BE LIKE THE MOST HI-I-I-IGH!"*

Gabriel could barely move. She shifted her eyes before her and saw a rock a few feet away. She used all the strength she had left within her and gathered herself to it. She tried to pull herself up but slipped. Gabriel cried out in pain as her body fell back to the ground; she was losing consciousness. Through heavy-laden lids, she could see Satan's flaming stare burning in her direction. A cruel smile spread across his face the moment their eyes locked. His tail rattled; he was headed straight for her.

Gabriel's eyes snapped open. Frantically, she reached up, grabbed hold of the rock and pulled her body on top of it. Her body racked in pain but she tried to focus her mind. Satan was closing in as he slithered across the ashen ground. With all the strength she could muster, she clasped her hands in prayer. Satan was almost upon her. Tears streamed down Gabriel's face as Satan threw his horns back. She cried to heaven, "GOD! PLEASE...HELP...*ME!!!*"

At the sound of the Father's name, Satan spit fire from his mouth as he threw his head down upon Gabriel. A piercing light from above suddenly penetrated the sky of hell shielding the flames from striking Gabriel. Satan roared and reared backward, blinded by the power of the light. The light radiated down upon Gabriel boring through her, healing her gruesome wounds, easing her pain — and then it was gone. In its place, standing between the devil and the archangel, was Satan's most-feared foe: *Michael* — and he was ready to battle.

Michael slowly drew his adamantine sword. He crouched in front of Gabriel like a tiger ready to pounce. Without a single turn of his head, he gave Gabriel the command, *"Run."*

Gabriel pulled herself up and raced forth into the depths of hell.

Satan growled. *"Michael*...you who were never worthy of the crown." Satan lowered his head and charged toward the archangel. He rammed his reptilian head into Michael, tackling him to the ground. Michael dropped his sword. They rolled until Michael was on top. Satan's tail wrapped around Michael's neck like a boa constrictor. Michael grabbed the tail around his neck and spun, knocking Satan into the Tree of Death. Satan's grasp was loosed.

Michael recovered his sword.

*   *   *

Gabriel ran through the Circle of Judas. Her crimson wings jutted forth from her back carrying her into the ashen sky. As she rose, she could see the center of the circle. The pentagram burning in its center lit the fire roads that led to all directions in hell.

She flew past the Valley of Homicides. Looking down, she could see the tar-filled marsh as it stretched for miles on end. The stench of decay rose up from the steaming bubbles that burst forth from the heat of the lava waves underneath. Gabriel covered her mouth, barely able to breathe in the toxic air that rose up from the blood-filled marsh. Deep moans sounded from the deep.

The giants: Goliath, Og and Sihon.

Having no desire to battle it out with the Philistines — Gokor's sons — she flew on toward the Onyx Mountains and reached the Valley of Slaughter. As Gabriel approached, she could hear the incessant howling from the hounds of hell. Their howling drowned out the woeful cries of the mortal souls in their domain. The valley itself was surrounded by caves formed from within the mountains. She looked down and saw the hounds' yellow eyes glowing from inside the caves. Their howling was like the wind on a moonless night. What they mourned over, Gabriel had never discovered. As they moved about the valley, Gabriel could see their reptilian-like bodies and dragon-like heads. They snapped and growled at the sound of a whip.

Asmodeus.

Asmodeus had dual whips in which he snapped at the hounds. They moved viciously toward a line of humans. They bit, growled and attacked the mortal men and women who had nowhere to go but take the abuse of the hounds as they attacked the humans like wolves during feeding time. Asmodeus' face lacked all emotion as the humans cried out, raged and seethed. Their teeth gnashed in agony, but there was no one to hear their woeful prayer.

Gabriel soared faster. The deeper she entered the inferno, the thicker the ashen rain became. She could barely make out the Onyx Mountains as she barreled through. As the fiery hail hammered down, it became harder and harder to fly. All around her, however, she could hear human souls being tortured, hounds feasting upon them, and fallen angels tormenting them amidst their screams and cries. *So many...too many...*

She flew past the Four Rivers of lava tide that led to Acheron and past the Woods of the Suicides. It was the most woeful place in hell. Each soul that took their own life had now become a tree. Looking down at the forest of human souls rooted in hell's grounds, Gabriel could see their eyes staring up at her. Their fingers reached up to her like intertwining branches. Their feet were planted deep within the brimstone ground; their legs were twisted and broken like the roots on the trunk of an ancient oak tree. Their eyes, wrists and throats bled incessantly, marking the wounds of the suicides. Seeing their bleeding eyes as they gaped up at her, hearing their gurgled voices attempting to speak through their blood-filled mouths, she lost the focus of her flight, and a large piece of hail slammed into the back of her head. She faltered. Her wings were hit again and again. She fell from the sky.

*　　　*　　　*

Michael slashed at Satan's side, dealing the devil a final blow that launched his serpent-like body into the Tree of Death. Colliding into the tree, Satan's horns embedded into the trunk. Before he could extract them, Michael took flight into the Valley of Darkness — the darkest, coldest place in hell.

Satan raged. He used all his strength from his wings to rip his horns free, but instead ripped the tree out from its roots. He rammed the tree against a rock until the wood was completely smashed, setting his horns loose. Satan roared to all the fallen angels, *"DESTROY THE ARCHANGELS!!! THROW THEM INTO THE LAKE OF FIRE!!!"*

From the Tower of Lucifer, the bells began to ring. Fallen angels all throughout the inferno heard the call of their master. They saw Michael fly past them. They spoke his name in whispers, *"Michael...Michael..."*

The sound of Gokor's elk horn sounded in the distance. The fallen angels launched into the blackened sky.

*   *   *

Gabriel crashed face-first into hell's grounds. The fiery hail continued to hammer down all around her. She fought to push herself up and came face to face with a frozen head. She cried out and scrambled backward but stumbled over more hardened mounds that covered the ground. She looked down and saw that they were all heads. Gabriel scanned the region; she was in a mine filled with them.

The Cold Ones...

Each of the heads stuck out of the ground. Their mouths were open wide as if screaming, but no sound came out. Their eyes, however, moved. And each of the heads shifted their eyes to Gabriel. She quickly stood up and whirled around, trying to get her bearings. She heard Gokor's elk horn in the distance. Fire poured all around her diminishing any hope of flight. She searched wildly for the mountains. She saw them up ahead. Gabriel took off into an all-out

153

run, racing across the field of frozen heads as she headed toward the mountain pass.

Felix slammed down onto the ground behind her. His red, goat-like eyes illuminated amongst the fiery storm. He searched the grounds. He growled triumphantly the moment he saw Gabriel up ahead. He raced swiftly after her.

*   *   *

Michael flew toward the valley. Deep within its caverns, there was no movement. There was no fire, no lava, no light. Not even Satan dared step foot in the Valley of Darkness, for one could lose their way amongst the shadows and the cold.

From all around him, Michael could hear the cackle of a woman. It echoed all throughout the valley. Michael searched all around for the sound, flying faster to reach a place of light. The cackle amplified within the valley. *The witch...the Witch of Endor.* He had forgotten she was there.

Michael's eyes illuminated, giving him the light he needed to fly to the other side of the valley. The moment he reached the last mountain, Michael came face to face with a squadron of fallen angels.

Instead of halting, Michael lowered his head like a bull and barreled through. Not anticipating this kind of response, the squadron was unprepared. Michael stormed toward them wielding his adamantine sword at the angels, striking them as he flew through them an beyond. The angels regrouped and followed.

Michael swooped and dove in and out of hell's domain as he searched for Gabriel. Hell's bells sounded all around him. He flew toward the Tower of Lucifer. The tower itself was molded out of the Onyx Mountains, stretching from the throne Satan sat upon to the top of the peak where the bells resided. Seeing them ring, Michael got an idea. A small smile formed on his face as he zoomed toward them. Taking his adamantine sword, he severed their chains as he flew past. The bells fell from the tower and crashed into the Lake of Fire, dissolving within seconds. He looked back at what was left of the heralding of hell's victories of welcomed souls and flew on.

From the ashen grounds, Gokor rose; Moloch and Azriel were right behind him. They headed for Michael.

*   *   *

Beelzebub was standing before the River of Christ. He turned his head back toward the Onyx Mountains. Hearing the bells suddenly cease their song, his blackened eyes narrowed in the realization. He looked up and saw Michael fly overhead; Gokor and a squadron of fallen angels were close behind. Beelzebub did not move from his spot. Instead, he turned his attention back toward the River of Christ that flowed down from the Kingdom of Heaven and into the Lake of Fire in Hell. His eyes scaled the river's tide and on toward the portal that led back into heaven. Its flow originated from the Great Waterfall in the second realm of heaven. *The portal that leads me home.*

Beelzebub bent down and took a rock laying beside his feet. He picked it up and stared at the river. He lifted his lifeless eyes, clenching the rock in his hands. He hurled it toward the river as high as it could go. The rock smashed into the portal, exploding against it. Small pieces of sand that were once rock, fell all around Beelzebub. He shifted his eyes toward the path Michael just flew. A small smile crept onto his face. *I wonder...*

*   *   *

Gabriel had reached the Onyx Mountains. She climbed its highest peak as fast as her strength could carry her. Beneath her, Felix rapidly scaled the mountain unseen.

Almost there...

Gabriel pulled herself up to the next landing when Felix was suddenly on her. He wrapped his arm around her neck in a chokehold and forced her off the mountain. They fought in midair as the force of the hail-filled rain hammered down upon them. Gabriel slammed her fist into Felix's nub. He roared in pain and released his hold on Gabriel. She lunged for the mountain and grabbed hold of a ledge and hung on. Felix slammed back on top of her, gripping her hair, trying to pull her back off the mountain.

Gabriel threw her head forward. The moment Felix was pulled toward her, she elbowed him hard in the face over and over in rapid succession. His one hand slipped from Gabriel's hair. The rain hammered down upon him, knocking him off the cliff. Gabriel hit the mountain and dislodged a piece of rock.

Felix tried to extend his wings, but struggled to do so against the hail. He lunged for the cliff and grabbed hold with his one remaining hand when Gabriel hurled the rock down upon his head. Felix slipped off the mountain again, but he grabbed hold of protruding rock sticking out from the side of the mountain. He looked up at Gabriel, his eyes were ablaze; he climbed. Seeing him rapidly rising, Gabriel turned and scaled the mountain swiftly, but Felix's movements were faster.

Just beneath her, Felix reached up to clasp hold of Gabriel's foot, but she kicked her heel hard against his hand. Felix roared in agony, but still held on with both his hand and his nub. He turned his hate-filled eyes up at her; they were glowing a fiery red. She kicked her heel down again, trying to break his grasp on the mountain, but he held on; she brought it up one last time and drove her heel straight into Felix's nub. That's all it took for Felix to lose his grip. He cried out in pain as he slipped and fell down the mountain, unable to rise from the hammering of the hail that carried him down the cliff toward the Lake of Fire. Gabriel watched the lava waves devour him as his screams died out; Felix was no more.

Gabriel was breathing hard, still staring down at the lake and its vicious waves of lava when she felt a pool of drool dripping slowly down her shoulder. She looked up and saw a demon directly above her. He smiled viciously at her with his grizzly teeth. The angel lifted his sword high above his head. Weaponless, Gabriel braced herself for the blow. But before the angel could slam it down on top of her, the angel's face was split in two by another sword from behind. The angel's body fell forward and into the lava waves down below.

Gabriel looked up to see his assailant; she recognized the emerald green eyes. *Vitor.* He extended his hand to Gabriel. She grabbed hold.

"I will fight them off as best I can." He handed her two of his swords from his sheaths. "Remember me when you speak to the Father next. Tell Him...*I'm sorry.*" She nodded. "Go...*quickly.*"

Gabriel could see the top of the mountain, the highest point in the inferno. She climbed.

* * *

Michael flew faster than he had ever flown before. He saw Gabriel climbing to the top of the highest, darkest mountain in the inferno. She reached it. He rocketed toward her, slamming down onto the mountaintop beside her. He saw her swords.

"You have weapons!"

She nodded. "Vitor..." Michael's eyes narrowed. Gabriel looked past him. "They're coming."

Michael turned. Like a herd of buffalo stampeding over the hills, hell's angels were closing in. Their number continued to grow as the swarm of angels rose and fell over the mountains. Michael pulled another sword from his back. "Gabriel, you're going to have to fight harder than you think you know how. On my mark...get ready to move."

She nodded. They stood back to back, wing to wing. Their wings intertwined and laced up, feather-to-feather, so that Gabriel and Michael were joined as one. With swords in hand, they raised their heads to the Father and prayed. *"Our Father...who art in heaven..."*

Gokor and hell's angels were one cliff away.

Gabriel and Michael lowered their heads; their eyes were enflamed with the fullness of God. *"Deliver us from the Evil One."* Michael roared,

"NOW!"

In unison, Michael and Gabriel spun into a ferocious tornado of light, rapidly swinging their swords at the fallen angels — slashing them, maiming them. The fallen ones collided against their swords; their bodies careened off the lightning strikes and blows that Michael and Gabriel dealt as they fought off the fallen ones. The archangels' light radiated upward into the sky of hell.

*   *   *

Beelzebub could see the light explode from the top of the mountain. He turned toward the portal; another rock was clutched in his hand. He shifted his eyes to the mountaintop; he waited.

*   *   *

Satan was coming up over the hill. He could see the tornado of light rising up to the boundary of hell's rooftop.

A portal.

The light set hell's sky on fire. Its force smashed into the boundary of hell; its lightning force wrapped itself around the portal and slowly opened its doors. Satan's eyes ignited in pure fury. He rocketed forward.

On Satan's approach, Michael saw him. He roared to Gabriel, *"FASTER!"*

*   *   *

Beelzebub watched as the portal opened. He took the rock and hurled it at the top of the river. It went straight through. Beelzebub's dead eyes suddenly came to life.

*   *   *

Satan saw the doorway. Raphael was just outside its opening. Satan watched as he reached down toward Michael and Gabriel. *"NO!!!!"* Satan was almost upon them.

Raphael grabbed hold of each of Michael and Gabriel's wings. Michael roared, *"PULL!"*

Raphael yanked with all his might. He pulled Michael and Gabriel through.

The portal closed.

The light was gone.

And Satan and the fallen ones smashed into the boundary of their domain. They fell onto the mountaintop, for hell's rooftop had been sealed by the hand of the Almighty God.

A PURPOSE FULFILLED

Gabriel was on the ground gasping for air. Michael pushed himself up, untwining his emerald feather from her fiery red ones. He turned to Gabriel and offered his hand to help her up. She grabbed onto it. As she stood up, she continued to grow until she had risen to her full height of over nine and a half feet tall. Michael gazed at her proudly, seeing the warrior of old.

My second in command.

The golden threads of her garments sparkled anew, her wilted wings were strong and vibrant again as they stretched forth from her back. Her scarlet feathers rattled as they shook off the ash from hell. Gabriel continued to dust herself off as Raphael walked over to her on tip-toe. "Here, let me help you with that." He dusted her off. "It's good to see you again, Gabriel."

Gabriel touched his face in fondness. "You who never doubted me."

Raphael blushed in reply. *"Never."*

Gabriel's face softened. "Thank you, my friend."

Raphael smiled, resting his hand over hers. "What is it?"

"Nothing." She dropped her hand from Raphael's face and turned toward her commander, "Michael." Michael's jaw clenched in anticipation of what she was about to say. "Michael, I wanted to tell you what I had done and why…but it was between the Father and me. Keeping it from you began to take its toll upon me, for that was the hardest part of my mission. It was killing me…"

Michael took a deep breath; a look of sorrow spread across his face. "Gabriel…I never…"

She put her hand up to stop him. "Satan watches me — *always*. To have you think me capable of falling to join his side meant that he would believe it too. And he needed to believe it to have God's will be done."

Gabriel searched his eyes. His face softened in understanding. "Michael, Prince of the Host, given the power of God to banish all evil that roams the world seeking the ruin of souls — you were just doing your job." Gabriel bowed with the greatest respect to her commander. She pounded her fist into her chest.

Raphael moved toward them and wrapped his arms around both of them, pulling them towards him. "Group hug!"

Gabriel looked at Michael. "He's been on the earth too long."

"Agreed. Raphael, let go…*I can't breathe.*"

"I don't want to. I love you guys so much."

Lightning suddenly struck across the sky. The archangels looked to it. Raphael released his hold. "Oh, great…another plague." Raphael looked behind him. His eyes grew wide. He ran off in sudden panic.

Gabriel looked to Michael, "Satan doesn't have my trumpet. The antichrist does."

Michael's eyes darkened.

"I had to be sure. Confronting Lucifer in hell was the only way to know."

Michael nodded. Raphael rejoined them; he was frantic. "I can't find Rachel."

Michael looked around for her. "She was with us when I crossed through the portal to hell."

"I know! She must have slipped away when the doorway opened again for you and Gabriel."

Michael was confused. "But why slip away now?"

Gabriel thought about it and then answered, "To fulfill her purpose."

*   *   *

The lightning storm continued to scrape across the sky as Rachel walked into the emergency camp. Looking at all the faces in the crowded tents, to the soldiers in military uniform, and at the civilians walking around in fear and worry, Rachel tried to focus her mind.

Think!

It was the trumpet they needed — Raphael had said so himself. So where was it? Michael thought Gabriel went to go get it from Satan, but Rachel knew deep within her bones that she wasn't going to find it there. Besides, Rachel had a part in this story to play, and she had yet to perform — that much was clear.

"I believe there is another being He has chosen for this task and it is not Michael, Gabriel or me."

Gabriel had made a point of singling out Rachel and demanding answers from her that put her on the defensive, as if Rachel were the one *with* the answer.

"What are you talking about? You don't even know me!"

It all started with Gabriel's knowing eyes when Rachel stood inside the Sistine Chapel. And it all came back to that question, *"What is your purpose?"*

How Gabriel's words tormented her. She felt like such a fool. How could one not know the purpose of their life? And even if she didn't know it, one had a choice on what it was supposed to be. And Rachel had thought she had made a pretty decent one — being a professor, keeping to herself, not doing anyone any harm. But Rachel knew deep down the archangel was not necessarily talking of careers. She was talking about something far more important.

Keep it safe.

At first she thought her father was only referring to the scroll since he had sent it to her, and maybe that is what he meant, but then she met Gabriel.

Gabriel did not say much, but the one thing she did say, she had shouted, *"You must know it! I know you do! For that is what makes you extraordinary in this dying world! You have to know it or it will all be for nothing!"*

What "all" was she talking about? Gabriel was God's messenger, and that was the only thing she ever said. So there must have been a reason.

"God has chosen his messenger well."

So what was she saying?

"Once the first tune was played, the spell — so to speak — would be broken and the devil himself could play the remainder of the tunes if he so wished."

"You should have known it was possible. If my father hadn't done it, the antichrist would have."

"The antichrist is a child born from hell. There is no victory in it if it were he. He has no soul to offer."

"Tell me about the antichrist."

And Raphael did. That was when she figured it out. That was when Rachel knew...he did have something to offer — *death*. And the only way to bring it was to play the tunes. It was the antichrist who had the trumpet, and he was here in the city. *But where?*

"My purpose, if I have one, is not to fix your mistake!"

And Rachel came to realize...*yes, it was*. She was not meant just to keep the scroll safe from the tunes being played, she was supposed to keep the world safe from the trumpet.

Standing in the emergency camp, Rachel was suddenly overrun by a sea of faces swarming in on her. She tried to free herself from their crushing embrace, trying to move away from the crowd until she realized she had backed herself into a darkened alley. She was suddenly all alone. She breathed in long and deep.

Too many people.

Rachel decided to remain in the shadows. Her hidden position gave her a perfect view of the camp and the people in it.

Put the pieces together. Solve the puzzle. Think back to the beginning.

Rachel thought back to when she first pulled the parchment out of the leather-bound case and all the events that followed suit up to this very moment where she found herself in an alley looking for a prophesy holding an archangel's trumpet. The day's events gave her no clues. All she knew was that she was supposed to be here at this moment in order to get it. She smacked her head in frustration, "Come on, Rachel! *Think!*"

Not a single neuron fired.

She looked out at the camp in front of her and felt utterly defeated. *Too many people.* The task was an impossible one. The antichrist could be anyone. There were a lot of important-looking people milling about the camp, especially the strikingly handsome man in military uniform walking through it.

Wait a minute...

She watched as everyone in the crowd parted like the Sea of Reeds to get out of this man's way, but they did not do it in fear but in absolute admiration and respect. He was welcomed with smiles and hands from everyone he passed. He smiled back at everyone and allowed himself to be touched by all. He shook hands with the old, kissed the heads of the young, and ordered the men under his command with one smooth unstoppable motion. Rachel thought to herself, *Now there is a man to be reckoned with,* for his eyes said, "If you get in my way...*game on.*"

"General!" The man stopped. He turned to the soldier calling after him.

General...

Almost as if he heard her very thought, Carter turned his head in Rachel's direction. She ducked further back into the alley hoping he had not spotted her. Unsure as to why that would be a bad thing, she did not know but relaxed a bit when he turned his attention back toward an old woman tugging at his elbow.

Could it be him? No, more people would be able to tell. Besides, he doesn't have the trumpet. This is impossible.

Rachel dropped her head with the feeling that she had given

herself too much importance to stop the inevitable. "God, I'm not one for believing in miracles, but if you could spare one, I could really use it…could you just…*give* me the trumpet?" She looked up to heaven and waited for a sign from God.

Silence.

She laughed softly to herself and nodded. "I know…that would be too easy. I'm supposed to move, do something…I just don't know what."

Rachel looked at Carter once again. "There's only one way to know." She decided to follow him. She moved toward the edge of the alley. A look of determination settled behind her eyes.

Lightning struck all over the sky.

Rachel jumped back at the sound of the thunderbolts, tripping over something on the ground behind her. She fell backward, hitting the ground with a loud *THUD*.

She pushed herself up onto her elbows. *What on earth*…She looked at her legs; they were draped over a metal box. Thunderbolts electrified the sky and gave Rachel just enough light in the alley to make out two carefully crafted cherubs carved on top of it. She moved her legs and sat up. Seeing that the entire box was covered in gold, Rachel ran her hands over the familiar angelic symbols. She cried out in joy. *"AAAA!!! The ark!* You see, Raphael. Sometimes, you *can* simply ask!" Her hands shook violently as she touched the cherubs. "Thank you, God!" She examined the angels. She ran her fingers over their swords and pushed them together. *Click*. The ark unlocked. She lifted the lid and saw the Trumpet of Armageddon inside.

*　　*　　*

"You told her why we were in the city, didn't you? When you told her about the antichrist?"

Raphael nodded, understanding Gabriel's meaning. "But she is without protection, Gabriel. I'm her guardian until God wills it no longer."

A beautiful light suddenly radiated down upon Raphael. He looked up to it, soaking in its brilliance. Michael also looked up, but Gabriel did not. She was more concerned with the changing emotions on Raphael's face. The light disappeared. Raphael dropped his head. "I'm done protecting her."

Michael placed his hand on Raphael's shoulder. "Just because you are, doesn't mean she is unprotected."

Raphael lifted his head. Michael looked at Gabriel. "Go." She bowed to her commander. More lightning struck across the sky.

Michael commanded Gabriel. "Hurry."

Gabriel lifted her head and nodded. An orange fire ignited behind her eyes. Her six phoenix wings jutted forth from her body. She nodded to the lightning, "I'll leave you two to handle this until I get what is mine." She vaulted into the sky and is gone.

As the lighting continued to battle the sky, the clouds began to separate. An explosion of light burst through the clouds. *Another portal.*

"What tune do you think it is this…oh no, not them." Raphael's face paled

"Yes, them — *the Four Horsemen.*"

THE FOUR HORSEMEN

The portal from heaven opened and the Four Horsemen of the Apocalypse rode through; each rider was on the heels of the other. The White Rider burst through the doorway first adorned in platinum armor.

Raphael stared up at him with disbelieving eyes. "I didn't know he had a rapier."

Michael took in the rider's weapon. "How else is he going to strip the world of food and water? That rapier will reap a massive famine." He studied the rider's horse. "I remember when he welded it."

The Red Rider was fast on his heels; he was wearing armor that mirrors the blackest night; a red cross blazed in the center of his breastplate. He carried a crossbow with arrows of fire.

Raphael's eyes grew wide. "That's your crossbow."

Michael crossed his arms over his massive chest. "Yep. I gave it to him after Daniel had his vision of the four beasts." His eyes glowed a fiery green as he watched the Red Rider — the rider of war. A look of pride rested behind his eyes. "I taught him everything he knows."

As soon as the Red Rider was through, the Black Rider barreled forth. Cloaked in darkness; his armor was the color of blood. An incense holder dangled from his side by a golden chain clutched in his skeletal hand. The smoke from the incense seeped into the air, forming massive cloud clusters amidst the lightning.

Raphael could barely speak, "That smoke will bring forth worse plagues than the ones the seven will wrought…that is the brimstone from hell."

Michael nodded, "From the Valley of Darkness…"

Lightning struck through the portal one last time…and the Pale Rider slowly came forth. He was dressed in a cowl made of a thin silky gray material. His armor was the color of sapphire and in its center was a star of gold. A sword rested across his saddle. He grabbed it and swung it high above his head.

"The angel of death."

He struck it down.

Raphael looked at Michael. "And I thought the inferno was terrifying."

Michael continued to stare up at the Pale Rider. "Death comes to us all. But when an angel brings it, only the gnashing of teeth follow." He shook his head, "His sword will hurl mortal souls into Hell just as fast as God's hand did when he cast our brethren out of Heaven. The horsemen aren't supposed to be here. They aren't supposed to come." Michael's jaw clenched.

"So what are we going to do?"

Michael did not answer. Instead, he took in each of the rider's horses. They were no ordinary horses. Their heads were those of lions. Their tails were not made of hair but were alive with snakes. The snakes writhed in fury, snapping their tiny heads with fangs loaded with lethal venom. Each horse's skin matched that of their rider — white, red, black and stone.

As soon as the Pale Rider crossed through, the portal closed. The riders lined up side by side as they hovered in the air. They were as menacing as the idea they represented: famine, war, plagues and death. The Red Rider looked down at the archangels. He nodded his head in respect.

Michael nodded back. The look on Raphael's face was one of pure dread. He shook his head, "Why couldn't he have played the tune for

bitter water? I could have handled bitter water."

Lightning struck behind the Four Horsemen once more. As it flashed across the sky, the thunderbolts created four pathways leading to the four corners of the earth. Each rider reared their horse to a single path of their choosing: one to the North, one to the South, one to the East, and one to the West.

Raphael pulled his sword from its sheath and took five quick breaths. His sapphire wings jutted forth from his body. "Okay, I'm ready." He took a step forward and suddenly stopped when he noticed Michael sitting against a rock. "Michael, what are you doing?"

Michael placed his hands behind his head, "Stretching my legs. Have a seat."

Raphael was dumbfounded. He spun his head back to the horsemen. "But...I..." He pointed to the horsemen. "I thought we were going to try and stop them from wreaking havoc upon the earth!"

"Nope. We're going to let them ride."

The four horsemen reared their horses and rode the lightning. Raphael turned back toward Michael. His mouth hung open in shock. "They rode! And we're not stopping them! I thought we were supposed to thwart them and protect all of humanity!"

"And how do you suggest the two of us stop the four of them from unleashing famine, war, plagues and death?"

"Through good old fashioned reasoning? Appeal to their senses?"

Michael shook his head. "It would take too long. They're incredible philosophers. Have a seat."

Raphael was so shocked he was utterly paralyzed; his mouth hung wide open.

"Raphael, don't worry. They won't ride far. Trust me on this one. We're just going to sit here...and let *Gabriel* handle it."

Michael closed his eyes. Raphael continued to stare at him in disbelief. He looked up to the lightning and spoke his internal thought out loud, "Gabriel is going to be so mad at us."

*   *   *

Rachel clutched the trumpet to her chest. She was breathing hard; her adrenaline was in flight mode. She crept against the wall. *You can do this.* She was at the end of the alley. *No one knows what you have. No one knows that you're here.* Yet, she felt like a bank robber all the same. *Breathe, Rachel.* She looked out in all directions to see if it was safe to flee unseen.

Too many people.

But the urge to move outweighed the doubt of caution. Thoughts of Raphael from moments before flooded her mind. Rachel sat beside him as he stood watch over the portal to hell. His hand rested on the scabbard of his sword ready to wield it if the wrong angel crossed the gate the moment it opened again. And there she was, doing nothing but sitting beside him, feeling like the third wheel along for the ride. She had never felt so useless and pointless in all her life. But how many times had she felt like her own existence resembled that very moment — like a bystander — never really living; merely existing. How many times had Rachel felt like she was on autopilot conducting the same routine in every hour of every day of her life — asleep and yet awake.

The moment Rachel laid eyes on the leather-bound case with its strange symbols was the first time she felt like she actually had a pulse. It was the moment where she was forced to swallow the red pill; and she was more than willing to do it, but this was not what she expected. She expected a reunion with her father long overdue, a family to belong to, and a future to look forward to all wrapped up in a leather-bound case. But her father was dead; she was the last in her family with no one else close to her or around her but an archangel. The rise of the plagues shifted the idea of a possible future to mere hope that there would even be one.

Come on, breathe.

Standing at the edge of the alley, she focused her thoughts, remembering the look on Raphael's face as he stood watch over the portal to hell — it was filled with confidence. Filling her mind with the strength he showed then was exactly what she needed in order to do what she was about to do now. *"You just have to choose to move…"*

And now it was time. *Move Rachel.* Taking a deep breath, she was about to step out from the alley when the cold wind blew. *"Not yours…not yours…not yours…"*

Rachel froze, too terrified to move. *That's what he wants. Keep going.* She clutched the trumpet tighter and shouted at the wind as it swirled all around her, lashing out at her with its whispers, "It's not yours either!"

She dashed out of the alley and into the crowd. She wove in and out of the sea of people, never looking back. *"MOVE!"* She shouted at people to get out of her way. Rachel immediately noticed the wind was gone. *Get to the cliff. Get to Raphael.* It was then that she heard a male voice shouting behind her.

"STOP!!!"

She ran faster.

"I SAID, *STOP!*"

Rachel could hear the pounding of feet behind her. All around her, people had stopped moving, but she continued to fly on by. The scenery all around her was a blur. All she knew was that she needed to get to the cave.

"DROP THE TRUMPET!!!"

She did not look back as the unknown man continued to chase her. Rachel continued to elude her pursuer. *It's him…it's him…it's him…don't…stop…running…*

As she ran past the shadows, all she could see were red goat-like eyes illuminating all around her. The shadows came alive as she ran from street to street, past the darkened streets. There was no electricity to help light her way. The shadows swiped at her from all sides. *"We hate…we hate…we hate thee…"*

Rachel screamed but kept running. The cold wind suddenly returned. It blew all around her, attempting to slow her run as she ran against its force. *Oh, God…*

The moment God's name formed in her mind, the wind swiftly disappeared. The whispery voices screeched in torment. Their eyes disappeared back into the shadows. Rachel slowed down. She looked all around the darkened street, terrified by the sudden silence. It was then she heard them...*footsteps*. She turned around and saw the shadow of a man as he turned the corner to face her. He stopped dead in his tracks.

"Put the trumpet down."

Rachel could barely speak. She shook her head. With barely a whisper, she uttered the words, *"No..."*

Rachel heard the sound of voices up ahead at the other end of the street. She turned her head to the sound. *Italian....human.* She looked back at the shadowed man, turned, and raced forth once again.

She passed the small trio of Italians walking down the street. She rounded the corner. *Almost there...*

Rachel knew that her life and the lives of everyone she knew, the ones she would never know, and the ones whose faces she had just raced past all depended on the success of this one single moment. *Run faster...*

Rachel headed toward the coast; her eyes zeroed in on the northern cliff.

There it is!

The moment Rachel reached the sand, a large being smashed down in front of her. Rachel screamed and fell backward. Her eyes scaled up the being as it rose to its full height of over nine and a half feet tall.

Gabriel!

Gabriel strode toward her with powerful steps. "Give me the trumpet."

Rachel was absolutely terrified. She continued to clutch the instrument to her chest. "You're so...*tall.*"

"Do not be afraid, Rachel. There is no time. I need the trumpet."

Rachel was too intimidated to respond. Gabriel crouched down to her so that they were eye to eye. "Rachel, listen to me. The Four

Horsemen are riding to the four corners of the earth as we speak. Michael and Raphael are trying to impede them from carrying out their stampede of destruction. I need my trumpet to call them off; that is the only way it can be done." She offered Rachel her hand again. "Give it to me — *please.*"

Rachel sat up and handed Gabriel the trumpet. The moment the trumpet was in the archangel's hands, it hummed softly. Relief washed over Gabriel's face as she held it. She looked at Rachel, "Thank you."

Gabriel stood and closed her eyes as she held each end of her trumpet in her palms. The trumpet lit up as a heat wave spiraled around it, cleansing it from all prior misuse. She opened her eyes, put the trumpet to her lips, and played its silent tune.

The tune sent out a sound wave that grew as it vibrated across the sand and sea and into the clouds above. Lightning struck all over the sky. An explosion of light burst forth. The portal from whence the horsemen came opened at the sound of the tune. Thunder rolled across the sky in response; it roared to the horsemen.

*　　　*　　　*

Michael and Raphael were lying on the beach. Seeing the lightning, Raphael slowly sat up. He watched as the doorway to heaven opened. Raphael looked back at Michael.

Michael nodded. "You see, I told you she'd do it."

Lightning burst forth marking the paths for the horsemen. And from the North, South, East and West — the riders came. One by one they galloped through the portal and returned to heaven. The Red Rider was the last to go through. He paused and turned his head back toward the earth. He looked down at Michael and Raphael. He pointed his crossbow at them. *"Soon…"*

Michael nodded. The Red Rider nodded back and headed through the portal. It closed and the sky went silent. Several moments passed before either archangel spoke. Raphael was still looking at the closed doorway when he finally decided to do so, "I still say Gabriel is going to be angry that we didn't even try to stop them."

"And who says she has to know?"

Raphael looked back at his commander, "Am I ordered to silence?"

"That you are."

Raphael laid back on the sand again. "Aye, aye, captain my captain."

*   *   *

Gabriel and Rachel watched the horsemen return through the celestial doorway. It closed and the sky grew dark once again. Gabriel closed her eyes in silent communication with her father. Rachel interrupted her prayer. "You knew I would figure it out."

Gabriel opened her eyes and turned toward her. She nodded. "But what I didn't know was what you would choose to do with that knowledge." A faint smile formed on Gabriel's lips. "That was a very brave thing you did, Rachel. Your mother will be very glad to hear the tidings, for it will bring her great joy."

Rachel's face stilled. "My mother? You mean...you see her?"

"All...the...time."

Rachel could barely breathe. "And...she sees me?"

"You are never as alone in the world as you think you are."

Rachel's eyes stung with tears. She touched her chest in grief and gladness as the emotions intertwined like vines within the garden of her heart. She looked up at Gabriel. "I...I owe you an apology, Gabriel. I have wronged you — thought you false — I even blamed you for my father's choice."

Gabriel put her hand up. "Peace, Rachel. We are sisters — you and I — each holding the other accountable for our actions and the actions of others — that is all."

Rachel shook her head. "Raphael was the only one who trusted you. He has such faith in your actions...I couldn't have done what

175

you did, Gabriel. Not even if God had asked me to…I couldn't have."

Gabriel's face softened. "I didn't think I could do it either. But I know that my Father would never ask me to do anything he didn't think I could handle. He knows my limits and does not push me past them or I would come undone."

Rachel was stunned. "You mean, you didn't want to do it?"

Gabriel's eyes bored into hers. "Facing the Lord of Hell is not something I ever want to do, for it forces me to remember things I would rather forget; and it pushes me back into the past, to a place I never wish to be again." She looked off into the distance. "But you have to do the one thing in life you think you cannot. And I didn't think I could do this, but it needed to be done."

She looked down at her trumpet.

"There are many things that I am asked to do, that I do not understand, but I choose to do them anyway — simply because I trust the one who asked. And I do not see the bigger picture in my Father's plans. I only see the mission — a mere glimpse of the plan. And it isn't until time passes that it all becomes clear as I look back upon the events that have gone by. And I am overwhelmed by it because it all makes sense. But this mission in particular was extremely difficult for me. I don't like drastic measures; I prefer simplicity."

"I suppose facing the devil in hell and burying the Trumpet of Armageddon was pretty drastic."

"So was retrieving the trumpet of an archangel from the antichrist." Gabriel smiled at Rachel. "You can see why I prefer things to be much more simple. But alas, everyone has a choice. And they don't always choose well."

Gabriel's face darkened. Rachel looked at the blood-filled sea as it continued to wash carcass onto the shore. Hail remained on the sand; small fires burned all around them. "You can reverse the plagues now that you have your trumpet, right?"

Before Gabriel could answer, a gunshot rang out.

Gabriel whirled around and faced the direction from where the shot was fired. A shadowed figure could be seen on the ledge above. The silhouette was human and looked masculine even from where Gabriel was standing. Her eyes narrowed in recognition. *It is him... the man without a soul.*

Carter raced toward them.

No, not *them*. He could not see the unseen. *He only sees...*Gabriel turned. *Rachel.*

Rachel looked at Gabriel. A large red stain widened across her chest as it seeped all throughout the fabric. She looked down at it. She looked up at Gabriel with terrified eyes.

"Gabriel..."

Her eyes rolled into the back of her head. Rachel's feet went out from under her. Gabriel caught her before her body hit the sand. She gently laid Rachel down and took in her pale face.

"Not yet..."

Rachel's eyes fluttered open.

Gabriel turned her gaze toward Carter. Her eyes narrowed in rage. Gabriel took her trumpet and swung it up behind her back. She rose to her full height, seething with wrath; she strode toward him as he raced forth.

I...see...you...

The veil was lifted.

Carter stopped dead in his tracks the moment he saw the powerful archangel barreling toward him. He tripped in the sand, falling backward. Carter scrambled, backpedalling as quickly as he could. All the while Gabriel advanced on him, her scarlet wings outstretched, her eyes blazing in orange flame.

Carter grabbed his rifle. He lifted it to his shoulder and took aim. He fired.

*   *   *

Michael bolted upright.

"Gabriel…"

His emerald wings rapidly jutted forth from his body. He vaulted into the air. Raphael was right behind him. They headed toward the beach.

*   *   *

The bullet went right through Gabriel. She continued to advance, never taking her eyes from Carter, never slowing her stride. Carter fired again. She continued barreling toward him. A ray of light shot down upon Gabriel from heaven.

Carter lowered his weapon taking in the brilliance of its glow. The moment he saw Gabriel raise her hand to it and rip a bolt of lightning from the light, his eyes grew wide. It was the first time he had ever known fear. Gabriel lifted her other arm up toward the light and pulled down her bow. She swung it down over her shoulder and aimed it directly at Carter's heart.

Carter's steely eyes locked with Gabriel's; he knew that there was a not a thread of opportunity to escape from this archangel. The look in Gabriel's eyes was confirmation that she had no intention of missing.

Gabriel was about to release her thunderbolt when Michael shouted to her from above, *"NO, GABRIEL!"*

She did not bother to shift her eyes but continued to aim her arrow of lightning at Carter. She took another step forward, but Michael dove down beside her.

"Gabriel…this task is not for you."

She stopped once again in encapsulated rage. She shifted her fiery eyes from Michael to Carter. Her voice was low and deadly, "You had better run, mortal man, for I don't always do what I'm told."

Bewildered, Carter took in the sight of Michael and Gabriel. He scrambled up from the sandy beach and, with rifle in hand, ran from Gabriel faster than he had ever run in his life. The moment he was out of range, Gabriel lowered her weapon.

Raphael landed on the beach. "Rachel!" Raphael picked her up in his strong, lean arms. *"Beloved…"*

Gabriel and Michael turned to them.

Rachel was extremely pale; she attempted to smile. "Raphael, I fulfilled my purpose. I found the trumpet…I didn't leave it unfinished."

He nodded. "You kept the people safe. What a mighty purpose indeed." He smiled proudly at her.

Rachel fought to remain conscious. "Tell me something…"

"Anything."

"Should I be afraid?"

Raphael shook his head. He smiled through his tears. "No, not ever, Rachel. For I know where you are going…and it is a place you want to be." Rachel's breathing slowed. "Close your eyes, beloved daughter of God. Someone is waiting for you."

Michael lifted his amber eyes and roared to heaven, *"OPEN THE GATE!"*

Gabriel pounded her fist into her chest at his command. Thunder rolled across the sky; a brilliant white light, brighter than the sun, exploded from the sky. The portal opened, but this time it was the Gate of Heaven that unlocked…*after all this time.*

*　　　*　　　*

The moment the gateway opened, the rest of the unseen world fell still. From the shadows of the city streets, from the gutters of filth, the fallen angels emerged. Gokor, Nero, Asmodeus, and hundreds of fallen angels slowly crept forth. They were absolutely paralyzed by the gate's effervescent glow. They knew that light. It was the light that bore them, loved them, nurtured them; it was the light that haunted them, for it was the very light of their home.

Home…home…home…

Gokor stared unblinkingly at the light. *"Father…"*

Nero was beside him, staring up at the light in utter bewilderment.

"Lucifer was right. God has finally come down to face us."

The moment Nero said their father's name, he growled. His burnt-red eyes narrowed in fury. "Yes, he has come to face his sons again!" Gokor pulled his battle-axe from his sheath.

Nero opened his palms calling hell's flames to them; they lit afire. "The gate is open. We can fly through."

Asmodeus cracked his whip. "I am ready."

Gokor gave the order, *"TO THE GATE!"*

They flew.

*   *   *

Heaven's light continued to cascade down upon the archangels, drifting past them, calling to the forgotten and the lost. From behind the archangels, Vitor emerged from the shadows. He walked toward the twinkling light, never taking his emerald eyes from it. "After all this time..." He fell to his knees and dropped his head in exhaustion and remorse. And he wept. He wept for the past, he wept for the present, he wept for the mercy only his father could bring. "Father, forgive me." Clasping his hands together, he pleaded his repentance. His body racked in waves of ancient grief, regret, and shame.

Hearing his song of woe, Gabriel was deeply moved. For she finally heard it: that single song of mercy, but she was looking for it in the melodies of the mortal world, and she found it in a fallen angel. She looked to Michael. Communication passed between the two of them. It was then that Michael's face turned severe. His eyes glowed a fiery green. He ripped his adamantine sword from his sheath at the sound of the soot-filled wings, the clawed march, the horrid stench of the dead.

The fallen angels had arrived.

Gokor, Nero, and Asmodeus led hundreds of fallen angels toward the portal. They were all armed for war. Gabriel gripped her bow tight. Raphael clasped Rachel tightly to him. Michael's voice was low and lethal, *"Wait."*

They watched as the fallen angels crept toward the light. And what the archangels saw was fear. *Terror.* The fallen angels waited for one of their commanders to move. Nero looked to Gokor to act, but Gokor could do nothing but stare at the light; he was utterly spellbound by it. He crept closer; he almost reached the light's edge when he suddenly froze. He breathed rapidly, taking in the height of the light as it touched the earth, reaching all the way up to heaven's dimension.

All the while, Michael and Gabriel waited, ready to battle any angel that dared step toward the portal of *their* home. Gokor nervously extended his burnt, scarred hand to the light. He almost touched it, then snatched it back. The other angels waited. Asmodeus nudged Gokor. "Touch it."

Gokor's eyes narrowed. He smacked Asmodeus away. He turned his eyes back to the light. He extended his hand once more. The moment his hand reached it, it was transformed. His burnt skin became pure and whole once again. His eyes grew wide. Gokor stepped further into the light. Gokor lowered his axe as both his wings were repaired in the light; their blackness turned to pearl; his skin and face were washed clean from the sulfur and ash. He closed his eyes, drinking in the light's embrace, breathing it in. The other angels were bewildered. Nero and Asmodeus slowly crept forth.

Gabriel gripped her bow tighter. Michael gestured his hand to stop her.

Nero's burnt skin was made smooth and luminescent; gone was the abscessed flesh and pain from the rawness of his wounds. Asmodeus' eyes were cooled and refreshed — turned from red to their sapphire blue.

The rest of the fallen angels slithered forth into the light. Their burnt skin and disfigured forms were made new and whole; they saw their former selves as they once stood in heaven: the most powerful angels of God's creation — the best warriors, minds, and ferocious hearts heaven had ever seen.

Clean…clean…clean…

Their agitated hearts were calmed. They breathed in the light; the light that they had been aching over for millions of years.

Gokor whispered the words, *"Father…"*

It was then that the light began to move away from them — Gokor and the rest of the fallen ones were blocked from its reach, leaving them in darkness once more. Gokor's wings returned to their single severed self. Nero's burnt skin returned to its painful, decrepit form, and Asmodeus' eyes were red and burnt once again.

Out of the corner of her eye, Gabriel looked to Michael. Without a turn of his head, he nodded to Gabriel. She looked to Raphael. Raphael rose toward the light carrying Rachel in his arms. Michael rose with him. His adamantine sword ignited in fiery blue. He rose alongside Raphael, guarding his ascent from the fallen ones. Gokor, Nero and Asmodeus watched the archangels rise up but did not attempt to attack — *just yet.*

As Raphael reached the gate, Rachel opened her eyes and looked up. Her face was radiant. She reached her arms out to the light like a child to a parent. Her body was lifted from Raphael's arms, and she was carried into the Father's embrace. Raphael and Michael entered the gate with her; they were gone.

Gokor seethed. His eyes never left Michael's ascent. He commanded his brood, "On my mark, we fly."

None of the demons remembered that Gabriel was still on the earth below. Crouched low to the ground, she slowly brought her bow around. She extended her hand to the light as she glanced menacingly at the fallen ones.

Gokor gave the order, *"NOW!"*

Gabriel rocketed into the air just as Gokor, Nero and Asmodeus leapt upward toward the Gate of Heaven.

Gabriel blocked their entrance and fired her arrows of lightning in rapid succession. She struck Asmodeus in the stomach, Nero in his hands, and Gokor in the forehead. They smashed back toward the earth. The rest of the fallen ones shrieked like frenzied chimpanzees at her sudden attack upon them — for she always attacked. They scattered away from the light and back toward the shadows of the city.

Gabriel clenched her fist tightly. She lifted it to the sky and slammed it down to the ground with a thundering clap. The ground quaked and a portal to the inferno opened. Gokor, Nero and Asmodeus fell through.

Gabriel moved toward Vitor. He remained on bended knee trembling violently in remorse. Sensing her presence above him, he lifted his head. The light from above poured over him. Soaking in heaven's light, his face transformed into its former self once again — his emerald eyes sparkled like the gems they once were. Gabriel looked to the light, hearing the command of her Father. She looked back at Vitor and said, "Go to Him."

Vitor's eyes shifted from the light to Gabriel. He froze, unsure if he really heard the words she had just spoken. Locking eyes with him she spoke again. "Go."

Vitor looked up toward the Father of Lights and slowly rose. As he rose, he was transformed into the angel he once was under God's creation. The light wiped him clean from his torment, from his remorse, from his shame. Vitor extended his brilliant ivory wings and raced through the gate. Gabriel watched as he crossed through the pearly gates.

She looked down at the portal she opened into the inferno. She crouched down to it and watched as heaven's light cascaded down into hell.

*   *   *

Satan stood before the Lake of Fire. Having heard the thundering clap of the portal opening, he looked up as the light fell all over him. He recognized it immediately, for the light was the light of his heart, his torment, his imprisonment, his home, his vengeance. His one reptilian eye dilated as the light rained down upon him. He raised his black horns to it, closing his eyes to breathe it in.

Satan's face transformed back into the mirror of his father, that of his former self — that of the Morning Star. From above he heard Gabriel whisper to him, *"Enlightened One...remember your purpose...you will never have heaven."*

His eyes burst open.

*　　　*　　　*

Gabriel swept her hand across the ground and closed the portal. She rested her hand over the sand and breathed in long and deep. *No, you will never see the light of our home ever again. There is a prophecy of old and it will play through as it was meant to...my...old...friend...*

*　　*　　*

As it closed, the light faded from Satan's gaze. His face turned back into that of the devil once again. He was left all alone in the darkness of his domain. Surrounded by nothing but the Onyx Mountains and brimstone beach, he raged, *"GABRIEL!!!!"*

*　　*　　*

Gabriel barely heard the beginning of Satan's cry as both the portals to Heaven and Hell were shut once more.

She looked up at the darkened sky and out at the bloodied sea. Taking her trumpet, she looked down at it for a long time. She ran her hand over its perfectly smooth horn.

"I've always had a love for the people of the earth..."

She looked out at the city beyond. Her six scarlet-colored wings jutted forth from her back; she rose into the sky. Bringing the golden instrument to her mouth, the archangel played a new song...and the world answered her.

THE RISE

Gokor, Nero and Asmodeus collided into the ashen sands of hell. Gokor immediately extended his wing and rocketed towards Satan's throne. He landed on the brimstone soil at the base of the tower and ripped the thunderbolt from his forehead. He threw it down in front of the devil in absolute rage. He screamed loud and long, emoting his frustration and wrath throughout the darkness in the fire world.

The Lord of Hell was unmoved as he sat on his throne, solemnly in thought. Unable to attract even a single glance from his leader, Gokor spit on the ground at Satan's throne and stormed off. He didn't make it very far before he was thrown into the air and held suspended over the Lake of Fire by the cold wind. He fought to release the grip of the invisible hand from around his neck. It was useless to do so.

Asmodeus was on his back; the bolt was still in his abdomen. Nero was on his elbows with the two bolts sticking out from his palms. They did not dare to move as they watched their fellow brethren hover over the lake of death. Nero slowly turned his head toward his master.

From the tower, Satan shifted his reptilian eye to Gokor. The moment his glare landed on Gokor, terror seized the gigantic cherub to the core. He recognized that look; and he knew that Satan would not hesitate to release him into the Lake of Fire to his immortal death. He hovered over it, suspended, unable to move. He looked to Nero and Asmodeus for help. With the slightest of movements, Nero shook his head. Asmodeus did not even bother to look at him; he was staring at the ground, hoping to be forgotten from this ill-fated scene. Powerless, Gokor waited for judgment from his prince — and then the judgment came.

With one swift motion, the thunderbolts were ripped from Nero's hands and Asmodeus' abdomen. The bolts rocketed toward Gokor. He screamed as the thunderbolts headed straight for him. Before they did, Gokor was thrown back down to the ground, spinning violently amongst the wind's force. The lightning bolts smashed into the Lake of Fire and were destroyed.

Gokor was on the bank of the lake — the lava just inches from his face. He crawled back away from it as fast as he could before the waves reached any inch of his skin. All three angels looked back at their prince. Satan had not moved a single muscle; not even a blink of his reptilian eye. Instead, Satan was looking out toward the lake as he did long ago when he first fell.

He rose from the throne, his snake-like tail slithering around him as he moved toward the lava waves. The angels scrambled to steer clear of his path. Satan stopped at the lake's edge and looked up toward Hell's Gate.

His eyes narrowed as he read its inscription: *"Through me is the way into the doleful city, through me the way into eternal pain; through me the way among the lost. Justice moved my High Maker. Divine Power made one, Wisdom Supreme, and Primal Love. Leave all hope...ye that enter."*

Satan looked at the massive gate. From the base he could still see the body parts of his fallen brethren when they first fell. Piled on top of them for miles on end, miles on high, human souls were interwoven to make up the foundation of the gate. He could see all the way to the top. His eyes seemed to darken the moment he saw the head of Jonathan Devereaux writhing amongst his fellow humans.

"Master…"

A red light from the earth interrupted this moment of joy and beamed down upon Satan. A man spoke from the portal above, *"My prince, the archangel Gabriel has the trumpet. She has reversed the plagues."*

Satan did not lift his head but merely watched the limbs writhe amongst the gate. "So…your first task, and *you failed.*"

The man was General Dante Carter.

"I am going to send Beelzebub to you so you do not fail again. Do what he commands, for the commands are my own. You have seven years to do what must be done. *Do it.*"

"Yes, my prince. For the kingdom…"

The red light was gone.

Closing his eyes, Satan focused on wiping out the sound of Carter's voice from his mind, for it was pure torture to him — for *he hates, he hates, he hates* mankind. But it was this one man that he would continue to tolerate and use to bring about his absolute rule over humanity. To know that it had been prophesized for ages that the devil himself should one day rule the earth in order to destroy it the way he had always wanted to is ironic indeed. To know that humanity anticipated it and that one of their very own would be the key to help do it — even now — gave Satan pause. *Why would the Father allow it?*

Looking up at Hell's Gate, he remembered it. He remembered it all. And in the remembering, Satan knew why God would allow any of it — free will. Human choice. Even in the depths of hell, he could hear his Father's voice saying to all of his creation, *"This day I call Heaven and Earth as witnesses against you that I have set before you life and death, blessings and curses. Now choose life, so that you and your children may live."* And he remembered that it all began with one man and one woman in a garden that mirrored the paradise of his making — Adam and his lady Eve.

"Brothers! It is to the players we go…"

One human choice.

Standing on the bank of the Lake of Fire, Satan could still hear

Adam's scream raging across the Garden of Eden when he realized what Eve had done — as if Adam himself did not have a choice in the mix. The fall of mankind was one triumph that Satan was most proud of, for it showed his Father one thing — *he was right*. What began with the fall of one had continued with millions. Hearing the screams of humanity here in hell with their woeful moans and gnashing of teeth, God must acknowledge the truth of it as well. How many more God would allow, Satan did not know. But the time was coming when he would find out.

Satan looked past the gate and slithered toward the highest cliff in hell where Gabriel once stood. He heard her voice in his head, *"Lucifer…the Enlightened One."*

Lucifer closed his eyes to the memory amidst the shrieks of pain, torment and screams of mankind in his realm of the inferno. The Lord of Hell breathed long and deep. *It's not over, Gabriel…it will never be over…*

I, GABRIEL

Gabriel crouched on a steeple in the Middle East; her trumpet rested comfortably in her hand. She watched the activity on the street below. And unlike the scene in the twisted play she saw before, the dialogue of this new day had written itself a new song. Gone was the gunfire, replaced by nothing but laughter. Gone was the chorus of bombs, vanquished by that of the most joyful prayer. Instead of tragedy, this theater now had melody. Looking at the people of the earth below, Gabriel knew this one thing: *the devil will never win his war, for the people of the world have always been worthy.* And she had been right from the very beginning: *she follows the Everlasting Shepherd.*

Gabriel rose up and soared toward Rome.

* * *

Gabriel landed on a steeple overlooking the main square. Thousands of people crowded together in anticipation of this momentous event: a new world order had formed and their newly-appointed president was about to be named. Looking at all the mortal souls below as hope spread across their faces as they waited to catch a glimpse of this self-made man, Gabriel breathed in long and deep.

It was in the beginning when God, my father, created the universe. The earth was formless and desolate. The raging ocean that covered the world was engulfed in

total darkness and the power of God hovered over its waters. In that moment, God bent time and space as he commanded, "Let there be light." And unto the light, we angels were born.

Gabriel watched as General Carter moved toward a large podium where numerous news crews thronged together. All cameras were on him as the entire world awaited. She watched with disquietude as he turned to face the crowd. *President Dante Carter.*

Created in His likeness and image, our father formed the Celestial Hierarchy, given free will to choose our fate: to stand in the light or fall into darkness. And some of our kind fell. It was then that God separated the light from the darkness, and in the light they were no more.

Carter began his acceptance speech.

Those who have ears, let them hear…angels exist in the world — both the heavenly ones and the fallen ones. When most people think of Hell's Angels, only one comes to mind. But there are many more than the one, and they all answer to him. And he wants you. All of you. He…sees…you…

The crowd erupted at Carter's words. They loved him, they welcomed him, they wanted more. And more they would get; more than they bargained for…

Gabriel looked across the way and saw Uriel standing on a steeple. He had the same look on his face that she did. He shifted his violet-colored eyes to her; silent communication passed between them as the crowd continued to cheer.

But we will not let him drag you to the inferno. For God has commanded us to guard you in all of your ways to lift you up in our hands that you do not strike your foot against a stone.

Gabriel looked down at the crowd and saw Michael standing amongst them. His muscular arms were crossed over his massive chest. The look on his face was severe as he stared at Dante Carter.

But through the centuries, we angels have become less important to the mortal world. Only existing in pieces of art, shrunk to baby cherubs, pretty fairies and pixies. But some of you have seen us…

Gabriel shifted her eyes to a little boy standing beside Michael. He was looking directly at her. His brown eyes glistened in joy as he stared at her in awe. She winked at him. A huge smile spread across his face. He waved at her.

Some of you have felt us...

Raphael stood beside an old man. The man looked beside him, staring straight through Raphael, bewildered by a gnawing feeling that he could not quite shake. Raphael looked at the old man and smiled his unseen smile. The old man shook his head and turned back toward Carter's speech.

But most of you do not know us, have never seen us, never felt us or believed that we could possibly exist. You believe that you are truly alone in the world.

The crowd exploded in jubilation once again. Gabriel looked back toward Carter — *the man without a soul.* He promised them peace, he promised unity, he promised them liberation. *Just like Lucifer did...the great deceiver.* Her eyes scanned the crowd. It was then that she saw him — *Lucifer.* He stood directly in front of Carter, staring up at him with a stone-like expression. Carter did not see his unseen master as he carried on with words welcomed by all.

You may even believe that you are no more than beings of mere dust and bone, filled with questions and receiving no answers that satisfy your thirst.

She watched Lucifer turn away from Carter and moved through the crowd. He looked at nothing and no one as he made his way through the sea of mortal souls.

But you are more than that. You are a mirror of the Most High God. You are His message, a verse on the page of His glorious plan.

Michael saw Lucifer move through the crowd. He turned and followed him; his eyes never left the fallen one. Sensing Michael's movements behind him, Lucifer shifted direction and moved toward the steeple where Gabriel was standing. His cerulean eyes scaled up its architecture until his eyes met hers.

Where there is darkness trying to blot you out from that page, there is the light setting the song of your soul on fire over the dark, burning your mantra into the history of time.

Their eyes locked.

Yes, there is evil in the world, but there is also a greater good that battles against it. Seraphim. Cherubim. Thrones. Dominions. Principalities. Powers. Virtues. Angels and Archangels. We surround you, cloaked by the veil of the unseen world. And when you call upon God for help, we will always come.

A smile slowly crept onto his face. Gabriel's eyes narrowed as she tried to decipher his satisfied look. Lucifer nodded to her and walked on toward the end of the square.

Gabriel jumped down from the steeple and stepped toward Michael. Uriel leapt from the building and landed on the ground beside her.

Uriel spoke to them, "Seven years from now, and it will all start again."

Michael's massive arms were still crossed over his muscular chest as he stood watch. His laser beam stare never left Lucifer. "Yes, Uriel, and the difference will be: we won't be on Earth then to protect the people."

Raphael moved through the crowd and joined them. He heard Michael's last word. "But that doesn't mean they will not be protected."

Raphael and Gabriel turned their heads to the crowd; the veil was lifted. Unseen by the mortal world were thousands of guardian angels standing watch over their human assignments.

For you are not alone…

The four archangels stood side by side watching the Lord of Hell as he walked into the shadows and stepped back into hell.

EPILOGUE

"*We are merely going to observe this day. Remember all that you see, all that you hear, all that you feel, for these are the things that we must use to our advantage…*"

Lucifer, Beelzebub, Gokor, Nero and Azriel flew past the adamantine gates of hell. There were two shadowed tunnels just outside the gate — the one that led to Earth and the one that led home. Lucifer looked to the pathway to heaven. He spoke to Nero, "Fly."

Nero's burnt wings extended; he rose toward the doorway home. A large green flame ignited the moment Nero reached the portal. He screamed in pain as he was rocketed back down toward the ground.

Lucifer's eyes did not blink as he stared at the doorway to heaven. "So be it."

He turned toward the pathway to Earth. Lucifer spoke to Azriel "Go."

Azriel did not move. "I…"

Lucifer whirled around at him; his blue eyes blazed in fury. "*Go.*"

Azriel nodded and slowly crept forward. He moved toward the shadows of the tunnel, readying himself for the green flame. He stepped slowly forth, inch by inch. He tensed, flinching in the expectation, but it never came. He continued on in the darkness.

Gokor stepped to Lucifer, "It is open. God is allowing us to pass through."

"That he is."

Azriel's voice shouted from the darkness, "I can't see how far it goes!"

Lucifer lowered his head like a bull; his eyes glowed in determination. "Brothers, *we fly*."

Each of the fallen angels' wings extended. They rose into the sky and headed forth into the darkness beyond. They flew, side by side, in silence as they continued on in darkness.

"Be on your guard, brothers, for this is too easily done. It may be a trap."

The angels nodded to Lucifer in silence.

For what seemed like eternity, they continued on in darkness until a small light appeared in the distance.

Gokor shouted, "I see it!"

They flew faster.

The light grew brighter the closer they got. The opening they flew through led them inside a large cave. The sound of a small waterfall rushing through it thundered in their ears. They landed near a small pool of water at its base. They looked down at the water and saw their reflections laid bare. Seeing their distorted forms for the first time reflected in the turquoise water, a flood of emotions washed over each of their faces. Taking in their burnt, scarred forms, they were paralyzed — the perfect mirrors of their father no more.

Lucifer turned away from the angels and took in the sight of the cave with its intricate markings and slopes — *so like the ones in heaven.*

Lucifer's mind was in overdrive; thousands of thoughts flood his mind as he saw the similarities to heaven all around the cave. He remembered his father's words and the excitement that filled his father's voice as he shared them with Lucifer, *"My Morning Star, I have created a place of paradise…"*

And here he was standing in a cave, bearing witness to mere words. He could not move and yet, he wanted to run through the cave to see what else lay before it.

"*Lucifer.*"

He turned his head toward the end of the cave.

"*Lucifer!*"

Lucifer snapped out of his dream-like state, torn from the memory of the past as he turned at the sound of Beelzebub's voice in the present. The memory of his flight to the Garden of Eden vanished from his mind's eye. Instead of at the waterfall on Earth, Lucifer found himself at the banks of the Lake of Fire, reminiscing before its deathly waves just as he did long ago.

"There is something you need to see."

"You're supposed to be with the Soulless One."

"This is important."

Beelzebub's black wings expanded. He rose and flew toward the River of Christ. Lucifer looked back at the Lake of Fire and out toward the highest cliff in hell where Gabriel once stood. He could hear her voice inside his head, "*Lucifer — the Enlightened One.*"

Lucifer closed his eyes to the memory amidst the shrieks of pain, torment, and screams resonating throughout the inferno. He breathed in long and deep. His six, opaque-colored wings jutted forth from his body. He rose into the sky and followed Beelzebub's flight.

* * *

Lucifer landed beside Beelzebub just before the River of Christ. "*What.*"

Beelzebub had a rock in his hand. He hurled it up as high as it can go. It exploded into ash the moment it hit the portal. "The portal…"

"What about it?"

"It opened when the archangels were pulled through."

Lucifer stilled. "*This* portal?"

Beelzebub turned toward his master; he nodded. "*This one.*"

Lucifer rapidly processed the information. "You're sure?"

A smile spread across Beelzebub's face. "Yes. When one door

closes, another one *does* open." Beelzebub watched his master's face, recognizing the look of deep, sordid thought. "You *were* right…God's weakness is that he loves. So do the archangels. They love one another just as the Father once loved us. What a shame it would be if another archangel were dragged into hell. They would never leave him behind — as we have so recently witnessed." Beelzebub lifted his coal-colored eyes to the portal above. "And the bells…"

"What about the bells?"

"The chains they hung from were made of adamantine."

Several moments passed as Lucifer digested Beelzebub's words. It was then that he realized all that Beelzebub had just revealed, and Lucifer's face turned from stoic to one of sheer joy. *"The prophecy…"*

And for the first time in billions of years, the Lord of Hell…*laughed.* He laughed long and hard; its sound echoed across the realms of perdition. Beelzebub, however, watched Lucifer's face the entire time without emitting any form of emotion.

"You need your sword." Lucifer's laughter died down as Beelzebub's black wings extended, "You have seven years to find it."

Lucifer's eyes narrowed. "Where is it?"

"I have no idea. Ask Gabriel, see if she answers…she…who never stood beside you." He rose and headed toward the portal that led to Earth.

Lucifer let him go, knowing the meaning behind Beelzebub's words. He looked up at the river's tide that poured down from the Great Waterfall in heaven, and he remembered it: the ever-changing sky, the sapphire steps, the manna falling from the sky, and *the music, the music* — home. A sharp pain pierced his heart. He closed his eyes in agony, clutching his chest as his hand rested over his faded star. It was then that he heard it: the echo of a woman's laughter.

Lucifer turned toward the Valley of Darkness. Looking at the darkness beyond, his breathing slowed. He hated that place. More than he hated the heat, the Lord of Hell abhorred the creature who resided there. He could hear the woman's laughter again. He cursed under his breath as he looked out toward her domain, *"She* would know…she would know where it is…"

Looking up at the portal to heaven one last time, still clutching the pain in his heart, he spoke silently to heaven, *Father…this story has not ended. It has only just begun. I will see your face again…*

Lucifer turned toward the Valley of Darkness; he was going to see the witch.

ABOUT THE AUTHOR

Corina Marie Zurcher is the author of the children's book *Growing Up Claus*, the Christmas book *Snow Falls* and the fantasy stories: *Archangels*, *The Father of Lights* and *Legacy*. She is also an actress, screenwriter, producer and the owner of RowanMeir Films. *Archangels* is the first book in the Archangels Trilogy and is the novelization of the screenplay.

You can follow Corina on Twitter, Facebook, and Tumblr. For all other information, visit: www.corinamariezurcher.com.